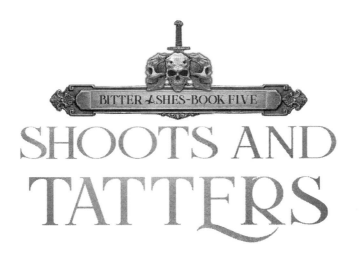

BITTER ASHES-BOOK FIVE

SHOOTS AND TATTERS

SARA C ROETHLE

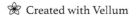

1

My eyes were glued to the television screen as I sipped my morning coffee, then rested the warm mug on top of my sweater-clad pregnant belly. I'd guiltily given in to the concept that since I was Vaettir, I could have all the coffee I wanted during pregnancy. Alaric sat beside me, dressed in a black tee-shirt and jeans, as enraptured with the news as I.

It had been two full months since I'd regrown Yggdrasil, the World Tree, and we still didn't know what to expect next.

The reporter on screen glanced at the destroyed building behind her. It had been completely overtaken by nature, which wasn't an odd occurrence, except that it had happened in the middle of the night, in downtown San Francisco.

This was only the latest in a slew of strange happenings since Yggdrasil had started leaking magic into the earth. Unfortunately, the humans had no idea *why* such strange things were happening. The most common theory was the apocalypse, though many others existed: aliens, bio-warfare, contamination from nuclear power plants . . . the list went on and on. There were even a few individuals who'd guessed correctly, that the old gods were preparing to return, making myth reality.

Now, we hadn't actually seen any gods yet, but we were pretty sure they were still coming, and we had no idea what we'd do when they did. Not long after we'd regrown Yggdrasil, I'd released the banshees from service. Part of me had wanted to keep them, but it wasn't fair to the tortured souls. Now that the gods' return seemed imminent, it would have been nice to have the extra protection, but I'd just have to rely on the Vaettir alone.

Alaric took my free hand and gave it a squeeze, drawing my attention away from the television as it flashed on more strange scenes.

I met his dark eyes, framed by his long black hair cascading down his chest. "I wish the old gods would hurry up and appear," I sighed. "I'd like to know whether or not they intend to kill me."

He took my coffee cup from my hand and set it on the low table in front of the couch, then grasped both my hands in his. "Whatever they intend, we'll be prepared."

I frowned, glancing around at the rest of the cozy living room, anything to not meet his eyes, lest he detect the fear lurking within my heart.

"I don't think the gods will have any issues reaching us in a simple house near the forest," my frown deepened, "no matter how many Vaettir stand in their way."

We'd moved shop not long after Yggdrasil had been regrown to be closer to it. While I preferred my hometown of Spokane, we'd found a nicely remote house halfway between Hilsboro and the desolate beach where Yggdrasil stood. We had plenty of tree-covered land to shield the less human-looking Vaettir, like Kira and Sivi, from the outside world.

Alaric's hand touched my chin, drawing my face back toward his. "They have no more reason to harm you than they do any of the other Vaettir. Try not to worry."

I shook my head, causing my long braid to slink behind my shoulder. "You know that doesn't make me feel any better. I don't want *you* to die either."

I looked down at my belly. I didn't want *any* of us to die. I didn't know what it meant for my child that I wasn't really human, nor was I truly Vaettir. Or maybe I was Vaettir, but filled with pure earth and death energy. At least, that was the conclusion Mikael had drawn. We didn't know *who* or *what* had brought me into being. Could someone unlikely to have been born in the traditional sense give birth to a normal baby, or would my child be just like me?

Alaric patted my knee, then stood. "Let's find Mikael," he suggested. "I know he has Doyen duties to discuss with you."

I smiled as I took his offered hand, struggling to my

feet. That he was suggesting we find his arch nemesis meant he *really* wanted to take my mind off things. If it was up to Alaric, Mikael and I wouldn't be working, nor living, together at all, but I'd come to trust Mikael more than most, so I was happy with the arrangement.

We left the living room, heading into the adjoining hall, then eventually the massive kitchen, done all in clean white and chrome. At the large dining table sat a few late breakfast eaters: Alejandro, Sophie, and Frode. With so many of us on different schedules living in one building, there was almost always someone sitting at the dining table. I was just glad this time it was three people I actually liked.

I glanced at each of them. Frode and Alejandro were like two sides of the same coin, both tall and muscular, but the former had pale skin and nearly white hair, while Alejandro's skin was a perfect bronze, complemented by hair as black as Alaric and Sophie's.

"Has anyone seen Mikael?" I questioned.

Alejandro and Frode both glanced at each other, their expressions hesitant.

"What is it?" I sighed. "You know I can sense your tension, right?"

Alejandro rolled his eyes. "Empaths are annoying."

"Out with it," I demanded.

Sophie sighed, flicking her straight, glistening hair over her shoulder. Something had happened in her blossoming relationship with Aila that had made her a total pill lately. "He's at the World Tree with Silver," she said matter-of-factly.

"What!" I exclaimed. Silver was Mikael's long-time associate, and had run Mikael's affairs in the states long before we arrived. I turned my gaze to Alaric at my side. "Did you know about this?"

He let my hand drop and crossed his arms. "If I had known, would I have suggested we find him?"

"Good point," I conceded, turning back to Sophie, Alejandro, and Frode, the latter of whom now seemed entirely focused on his food, his thick, white blond hair falling forward to obscure his strong, Scandinavian features.

"How long ago did he leave?" I asked the trio.

Alejandro shrugged, flexing the muscles in his bare shoulders beneath his white tank top. "About thirty minutes, give or take, but we can't let you go after him."

I tugged up my too-loose maternity jeans, then crossed my arms above my round belly. "Oh? And how are you going to stop me?"

Alejandro smirked. "Don't make me wrestle a pregnant woman."

"You'll have to go through me first," Alaric purred, moving to stand a few paces ahead of me.

"And me," Sophie added, casually scraping her fork across her plate.

Alejandro and Frode simultaneously turned to Sophie. "But you agreed to keep her here," Frode balked.

She smirked. "Just like I agreed not to tell her where

Mikael went. Really, it's astounding how dense you all are. I'll always side with my brother and the mother of my soon-to-be niece."

Alejandro and Frode both scowled at her.

"Well now that that's settled," I concluded, turning to Alaric, "Shall we?"

He nodded, then flicked his gaze to Sophie.

She shook her head. "Don't look at *me*, the World Tree gives me the creeps."

I shrugged. "Fair enough."

I took Alaric's hand and turned to go, while Alejandro and Frode muttered behind us about how much it sucked to have me as a co-Doyen with Mikael.

In truth, I knew they were alright with me assuming the role. They were smartasses, but genuinely good hearted enough for me to consider them friends. I couldn't blame them for being a little upset that Mikael would put them in a tough spot with me.

Our hands still joined, Alaric and I walked past the closed front door, continuing straight toward the six car garage.

Alaric held the interior door open for me while I reached in and hit the lights, then stepped inside to retrieve my keys from the hook on the wall.

The keys belonged to a four-door, silver Ford F150, not really my first choice in vehicles, but the four-wheel drive came in handy on the long, often muddy driveway.

Alaric went around to the passenger seat while I climbed into the driver's side, using the interior handle for leverage as I labored myself into place. I'd gotten used to not driving myself around for the most part, but when it was just Alaric and I, I drove. He was capable, but since he'd lived most of his life in the various Salr, sanctuaries of the Vaettir, he hadn't needed to drive frequently enough for it to become a habit.

I pushed the garage door button fastened to my sunshade, waited as it opened, then backed out and we were on our way, too late for Alejandro and Frode to change their minds and try to stop us.

Once we were halfway down the muddy driveway, surrounded by tall fir trees obscuring the murky sky, I finally asked, "What do you think they're doing at the World Tree?"

Alaric shook his head, his silky black hair nearly shimmering. Silky like a cat's pelt, which made sense since Bastet was the goddess from whom he descended.

"Trying to figure out why the gods haven't plunged down to punish us all?" he questioned.

I nodded, having come to the same conclusion. "I can't believe Mikael went without me," I muttered, slowing the truck to avoid a deep rut in the road. "This matter concerns *me* more than most. I should have at least been informed."

Alaric sighed. "Mikael may be a scoundrel, but he *does* care about your well-being. I'm sure he's only trying to protect you."

I scowled. "I'm a big girl."

He chuckled, glancing at my belly. "Yes, you are."

I sighed, keeping my eyes on the drive. "You're incorrigible."

I turned the truck off the driveway and onto the paved street, sparsely lined with other enormous houses, and a few farmsteads. Eventually the road ended with a turn, then another onto a small highway that would lead us to the place where Yggdrasil had taken root. Normally, a giant, golden-branched tree in the middle of a desolate beach would seem out of place, but it was a magical tree perceivable only to magical folk . . . at least for now.

With magic leaking into the mundane lives of humans at an alarming rate, it was only a matter of time before someone was affected by enough magic to be able to see the tree. We hoped to have everything sorted out with the gods well before that point.

Alaric reached across the center console to place his hand on my thigh, a familiar, comforting touch.

Even though I was terrified of what the gods might do, that simple touch brought me peace. We would defy the odds together, just like we'd been doing from the start. Not the gods, mischievous Vikings, nor the hoard of Vaettir under our command would stop us.

IT TOOK us twenty minutes to reach the beach where Yggdrasil had sprouted, and since Mikael and Silver had left thirty minutes prior, it meant they'd had our entire drive plus some to cause trouble.

Having driven on a narrow forest road right up to the edge of the beach, I parked the truck and stepped out, with Alaric mirroring me on the other side.

"There they are," he pointed as he reached my side.

In the distance I could see the tall, golden branches of Yggdrasil, reaching endlessly up toward the cloudy sky, and below them, the forms of two men. I couldn't see their features from such a far distance, but I could recognize Mikael by his height, roughly 6'5" and his long, rich, auburn hair, and Silver, just a few inches shorter, with short black hair shiny with gel.

I took a moment to sense our surroundings, then shuddered. "I feel magic."

Alaric glanced at me, then back toward the men on the beach. "Is that so unusual this close to the World Tree?"

I shook my head. The sound of the nearby ocean seemed overly loud to my ears. "No, but I sense *more* of it. We need to get down there and see what they're up to."

Alaric nodded. "Shall I run ahead?"

"Yes," I decided, my gut clenched tight with worry.

Unfortunately, I was human slow on a good day, and with my ever growing belly, I was even slower. Alaric would be able to reach them in seconds.

He gave my shoulder a squeeze, then took off ahead of me, his black jeans and tee-shirt turning him into a dark blur bounding across the beach.

I waddled after him, far less graceful. I couldn't help but be grateful no one was left behind to watch.

9

I kept my eyes on my footing, glancing up every so often until Alaric reached them. The chill wind rolling in from the ocean pushed tendrils of my long hair back from my slightly sweaty face. I wrapped my arms tightly around myself, trying to quiet my breathing enough to pick up hints of conversation carried across the wind. I could hear the murmur of male voices, but was still too far to decipher what they were saying over the gentle crash of the tide.

I continued waddling, kicking up sand with each step. I could feel the magic increasing, seeming to stem from Yggdrasil. It wasn't like this the last time we'd visited. Mikael and Silver had done . . . something.

I was close enough to catch a few words of heated conversation when Alaric turned in my direction.

"Go back!" he shouted.

I stopped for a moment, perplexed, then continued walking forward.

Mikael turned as I neared them. "Madeline, go back right this instant," he demanded.

"Like hell!" I snapped. "I'm not going anywhere until someone tells me why this beach feels like it's about to explode with magic."

As soon as I reached them, Alaric put his hands on my shoulders, attempting to drive me back in the direction I'd gone.

"They're trying to summon one of the gods," Alaric explained as he gently pulled me away. "And it seems to be working."

I stepped out of his reach. "Why would you summon them without me?" I demanded, staring Mikael down.

Silver continued to gaze up at the tree, his chiseled features and hooded eyes slack. "Something is coming," he muttered.

With a huff of exasperation, Alaric lifted me into his arms like a child. He started to turn away, then the tree began to glow with golden light, just like it had when it first took root.

"Huh," Mikael observed. "It's *actually* working."

The building magic suddenly climaxed, and a burst of light appeared at the tip of one branch, then shot rapidly down the tree. Once it reached the base, a male figure began to form.

Mikael glanced back at me, concerned, though he couldn't blame me for not running away, as it was Alaric's feet that stood still.

We all turned back to the golden light figure as it solidified into a man. He stepped forward out of the glare. Long red hair, several shades brighter than Mikael's, trailed over his shoulders. His clothing was reminiscent of what we'd worn when we traveled back in time to meet with Vikings, only far finer. His blue linen tunic was embroidered with elaborate golden designs, and his black pants and boots appeared finely crafted by hand.

"Dolos?" Mikael questioned.

The man, handsome in a lanky, angular sort of way, smirked. "Hardly." He glanced around at each of us, his gaze settling on me, still cradled in Alaric's arms. "Well aren't *you* an odd sight," he mused, taking a step forward. "Like a little ball of brilliant death light."

"Brilliant death light?" I questioned, my jaw going slack.

"Who are you?" Alaric asked from above me.

The man bowed with a sarcastic flourish, then straightened. "My apologies, it's been quite some time since I set foot on Earth. You may call me Loki."

"Holy shit," Alaric gasped.

Loki raised an eyebrow at me. "Not the most eloquent man in the world, is he?"

I found myself without words. Meeting the Morrigan was one thing. Facing down Loki, Norse god of mischief, was quite another.

Holy shit indeed.

2

"How did this happen?" Mikael questioned. "None of us are descended from you."

"And who are you descended from?" Loki asked smugly.

"Dolos," Mikael replied.

Loki kept his eyes on me as he answered, "Same energy," he gestured down at his lanky body, "different incarnation."

I tapped Alaric's arm. "Care to let me stand?" I whispered.

Still seemingly stunned, he obeyed. He'd been willing to cart me away from a glowing tree, but carting me away from a god was probably a bad idea. Didn't want to piss off the ancient, omnipotent being.

"I think it's like with the Morrigan and Hecate," I explained hesitantly, giving Loki a wide berth to approach Mikael. Loki slowly turned to keep his eyes on me, a smirk lifting the corner of his thin lips. "They were entirely different women," I continued, "but their energies are similar, just like—"

Lightning fast, Mikael shot behind me and sealed his hand over my mouth. After a second of being pissed, I realized why he'd taken such action. I'd almost admitted to a *god* that I wasn't like other Vaettir, by admitting I was inhabited by the same energy that created the Morrigan.

Loki watched us curiously. "The Morrigan, you say?" He stroked the reddish brown stubble on his chin. "*Now* it all makes sense." He paced across the sand, flicking up granules with his boots. "I was debating whether or not to come at all, then I sensed the big glowing death ball," he gestured to me, "and had to see what it was."

I looked down at my round belly, wondering if he was making a pun. Did gods make puns?

Loki turned his gaze out toward the ocean, watching it thoughtfully.

As Mikael fully released me and Alaric sidled up next to us, I realized someone was missing. "Where's Silver?" I whispered to Mikael.

"Cowardly bastard," Mikael sighed, flicking his gaze to Loki, then to the beach behind us, boasting the telltale footprints of Silver's escape.

I tried not to laugh. It probably would have come out hysterical given my anxiety at having a god who might want to kill me standing before us, but it *was* funny. Silver had high-tailed it when I'd summoned my banshees too. It was no surprise he'd take off in the presence of someone like Loki.

Loki turned back to us, aiming his eyes at me. "You know, we should probably leave this place before one of the other gods senses you. There are some who would debate you should not exist." He looked me up and down. "You're just so *shiny*."

Crap. We were right after all. I was an anomoly, a freak of nature. I wasn't supposed to exist and each of the gods would know it as soon as they saw me.

"But you believe she should?" Mikael questioned.

Loki tilted his head as he continued to observe me. "Well she's interesting, and doesn't *immediately* make me want to squash her like a bug."

I took a step back. Maybe I should have run while I had the chance.

Loki crossed his arms and tapped his foot in the sand, seeming to ponder keeping me alive.

"I'll tell you what," he said after a moment, unfurling his arms. "Let's get off of this desolate beach and back to civilization, have a nice meal, and we can discuss your existence over a nice glass of wine."

I gulped. He seemed to be speaking just to me, so it was probably my job to answer.

I didn't relish the idea of taking him back to civilization, but if we could convince him to be on our side . . . "Umm," I hesitated, "Okay?"

He clapped his hands together. "Brilliant. Now let's be off before the other gods catch us."

He walked past us in the general direction of the truck.

I glanced at Mikael, then Alaric.

"*Okay?*" Alaric mouthed, clearly not pleased with my decision.

"What else was I supposed to say?" I hissed.

"Perhaps we should follow him," Mikael interrupted, gesturing further down the beach to where Loki walked.

We started forward at a brisk pace to catch up with him to show him the way, but there was no need. Following my previous footprints in the sand, he veered toward the truck concealed in the trees.

Mikael and Alaric matched my slow pace. Even so, I was a bit breathless by the time we reached Loki to find him leaning against the silver exterior of the truck.

"Not my first choice in vehicles," he muttered, clearly offended by the truck.

"I'll drive," Mikael offered, holding out his hand for the keys.

"Yes," Loki agreed, "then the death ball and I can sit in the back."

"*I'll* sit in the back with Madeline," Alaric stated, boldly arguing with a god.

I held my breath. I didn't want to sit in the back with Loki, but I also didn't want to anger him.

Loki simply smirked, looked Alaric up and down, then replied, "As you wish, Kitty Cat."

I nearly choked on my own spit at the name. It was exactly what Mikael liked to call Alaric, mockingly.

Mikael didn't seem to notice, however, and simply took the truck keys I'd pulled out of my pocket and unlocked the vehicle.

I glanced at Alaric, then climbed into the back seat behind Mikael, scooting over to make room for Alaric to climb in after me.

Loki walked around the vehicle, opened the front door, then situated himself in the passenger seat, delicately shutting the door behind him.

As soon as Mikael started the ignition, Loki began to fiddle with the temperature and radio knobs.

"How do you even know what a vehicle is?" I asked, unable to help my curiosity.

Loki turned to arch a red brow at me. "I reside in an alternate plane, not *Middle-earth*."

I narrowed my gaze as I thought over his answer.

Mikael carefully backed the truck out between the trees, snapping small branches and fir needles beneath the tires, then began driving back the way we'd come. I didn't see what vehicle he and Silver had arrived in, but assumed Silver must have taken it when he fled.

Loki turned back around to fiddle with the radio knobs some more, flicking through the stations before finally turning the music off altogether.

Soon enough we were back on the highway. Alaric and Mikael were both acting like we didn't have a *god* in the passenger seat. Maybe they'd both lived long enough that it wasn't exciting, but I still couldn't quite contain myself.

"So you said you live in an alternate plane?" I blurted. "How exactly does that work?"

Loki turned in his seat to look at me, while Alaric gave me a *what the hell are you doing?* look.

"I'll answer one of your questions," Loki teased, "if you answer one of mine."

"No, thank you," Alaric answered for me.

I scowled at him, then turned back to Loki. "You ask your question first. If I don't want to answer, then you don't have to answer mine."

"Deal," he agreed, as Alaric let out a heavy sigh.

Still turned toward me, Loki tapped a finger against his lower lip, thinking, then asked, "Where did you come from? Were you born . . . normally?"

My shoulders relaxed. He already knew I wasn't normal, so answering that question wouldn't be giving too much away, especially since I didn't actually know the answer.

"I always thought I was born normally," I replied, "but now I'm not sure. I grew up in foster care, not knowing I belonged with the Vaettir. Now that I've found them, no one seems able to tell me who my parents are."

"Interesting," he replied, his blue eyes thoughtful.

I shrugged. "If you say so. Now, my turn."

"The plane I live on is more primitive than this one," he explained, "but only because we have access to more magic. There is less need for technology," He seemed to think for a moment, then continued, "I'm not sure how to explain alternate planes to mortals. There are many worlds you do not know about. The beings in these worlds exist in this same span of time ... and not. Time is anything but linear. You are, in fact, existing in the same time as your ancestors, just in a marginally different plane."

I nodded. I'd come to accept I'd never truly understand time and different planes after traveling back to meet the Vikings, then even further back to see the World Tree where it originally stood. Perhaps I hadn't traveled *back* at all. Maybe I'd gone parallel.

"That's interesting," I concluded, "but I've changed my mind about my original question."

He smirked. I'd assumed he'd wave me off and say my first question still stood, but he only gestured for me to go on.

"Okay," I breathed, thinking my words through before I said them. "You claimed some gods would want to destroy me. I'm assuming you don't, since I'm still alive. My question is who will want to destroy me, and *why*?"

"Good question," he encouraged, making me feel more relaxed as Mikael sped down the highway. "The who isn't terribly relevant, and I cannot say for sure. All I can say is that your odds with any god are about fifty-fifty. As for the *why*, you're a bit of an abomination. You should not exist in a world that is mostly devoid of magic. Some will stop with the reasoning right there. It is the task of the gods to maintain natural balance. Threats to that balance," he gestured toward me, "must be eliminated."

I bit my lip, then pressed, "But you don't want to eliminate me?"

He shook his head. "No, at least not yet. I'd rather like to see how this all plays out. Plus, for any who argue that you upset this balance, there will be others who say you *keep* it. That your energy belongs on this Earth."

"So half the gods won't want to destroy her," Alaric interrupted, "because maybe she belongs here?"

Loki flicked his gaze to Alaric. "She regrew Yggdrasil, at least, I assume it was her. The tree now reeks of her magic. Some might presume that fact means the gods and magic *should* return to this plane. If we are meant to return, then perhaps she's *supposed* to be here."

I mulled over his words, then asked, "So you want to help us because you want the gods to return to this plane?"

He tsked at me. "Now, now, you're not playing fair. I've only gotten to ask one question this entire conversation."

"Well, ask your next one quickly," Mikael advised, "we're almost home."

Before Loki could ask anything, Alaric interrupted, "Are we sure we want to take him *home*?"

Loki rolled his eyes. "I'm housebroken, I assure you."

I snorted. "There are more of the Vaettir at . . . home. If we bring you there, we'll have to reveal to everyone that one of the gods has returned. They might panic."

Loki turned his attention to Mikael. "That sounds tiresome. Take me somewhere nice to eat instead."

"Fine," Mikael answered simply.

He was being unusually quiet, and I wondered why. I could sense his tension, but heck, we were driving down the highway with a god in our vehicle. All three of us were tense.

"I should at least call Sophie," Alaric muttered.

"And tell her the truth?" I questioned.

He leaned to the side and pulled his cell out of his pocket. "She knows how to keep her mouth shut." He smirked. "At least when *I* ask her to."

"So we won't be telling anyone else?" I asked.

Loki had turned back around to watch our conversation curiously. Alaric glanced up from his phone to him, his thumb on Sophie's name in his contact list.

"Is that alright with you?" Alaric asked, seemingly unable to interpret Loki's gaze.

Loki nodded. "Keep me a secret if you please. We can concoct an identity for me over lunch."

It was all well and good to make Loki a new identity, but there was still one issue. "I think some of the others might be able to sense his godly...magic," I shared. "He doesn't *feel* like one of the Vaettir."

There was a shift in pressure in the car, though no one moved.

Loki asked, "There, how do I *feel*," he drew out the word to make it sound dirty, "now?"

I glared at him. He really was cut from the same cloth as Mikael. Entirely incorrigible.

"You feel like a human," I stated blandly. "I don't sense unusual energy from you at all."

Loki pursed his lips, clearly displeased. "I've never had to disguise myself as one of the Vaettir before. You only exist on the timelines of this particular plane."

He placed his hand on my knee, then his energy shifted again.

I turned my legs to the side, pulling them out of his reach. "I'm not even truly Vaettir. Touch one of *them*," I gestured between Alaric and Mikael.

"Fine," he pouted, turning further to place his hand on Alaric's knee instead.

Alaric tensed beside me, but did not pull away.

"Better?" Loki asked, retracting his hand.

I focused on him, letting his energy seep into my senses, then nodded. "Better. You feel like one of the Vaettir now, although, some can tell our race through scent." I turned my gaze to Alaric.

He rolled his eyes. "He smells like one of us now too."

Loki laughed and clapped his hands together. "Marvelous. You are a perceptive lot."

He turned forward in his seat as Mikael entered the lunch time traffic heading toward Hillsboro.

Alaric turned his attention back to his phone and dialed Sophie's number. After a brief argument where Sophie was obviously irate over not knowing what was happening, even though it had only just happened, he pulled the phone away from his ear.

"Where are we going to eat?" he asked, his attention on Mikael's back in the front seat. "Sophie wants to meet us."

I rubbed my belly as it growled. "*Angelo's?*" I suggested, though no one was asking me. "I think I might die if I don't have pasta," I paused, focusing my thoughts on food, "and a grilled cheese," I added. "And ice cream."

"That sounds delightful," Loki agreed.

Alaric sighed, then pressed the phone back against his ear, relaying my choice to Sophie.

I relaxed against my seat as he hung up the phone, hoping that Loki finding us was a good thing. Surely someone who seemed so laid back wouldn't just suddenly change his mind and kill me.

I glanced at Loki out of the corner of my eye. He seemed to be preoccupied with reading the street signs as we entered the outskirts of Hillsboro. I went over everything I knew about him, wondering if we could trust him. I knew he was a trickster god, and if he shared the same energy of Dolos, he was a master manipulator and diplomat.

The only question was, why would he want to manipulate *us*, and to what end?

TWENTY MINUTES later we'd parked the truck and were walking into Angelo's, a quaint Italian bistro in downtown Hillsboro. Their food was always good, yet they were somehow never too busy.

As soon as we entered the dimly-lit establishment filled with old world decor, we were seated at a large booth with a heavy wood table. Alaric immediately slid into the booth after me, leaving Mikael to sit beside Loki.

I watched Mikael's somber expression, looking for some sign to the why of his sour mood. He'd been trying to summon a god, after all, and he'd gotten one. I didn't see what difference it made which god we got, as long as it was one who didn't want to kill me.

Our waitress, a teenager with shortly cropped blonde hair and a nose ring, came to take our orders. I didn't miss the way she looked each of the men at the table up and down, though there was a hint of apprehension to her energy. I supposed they were quite the trio, all tall with long hair, and with Loki dressed in his fine, but dated, garb.

I was about to order a grilled cheese with a side of spaghetti, then thought better of it and ordered mushroom ravioli and garlic bread, coffee too. Loki ordered half the menu, along with a bottle of red wine, and the other two men ordered nothing.

We all sat in silence for several minutes as Loki peered around the establishment, his gaze lingering on the bar at the other side of the restaurant.

"So," Loki began, shifting his gaze to me, "let us

continue this question game. I believe I'm owed at least two prompt answers at this point."

I stared at him, not sure if I should continue the game or not.

Seeming to take my silence as an answer, Loki began, "You claimed to have interacted with the Morrigan in the past. Have you had any contact with Hecate, or any of the other death goddesses?"

I glanced at Alaric, wondering if I should tell the truth.

"I suppose it can't hurt," he muttered.

I bit my lip, wishing I had a glass of water or coffee to fiddle around with, but the waitress was yet to bring them. She'd probably been too busy deciding whether she should ask one of the men for a date, or run the other way. "I haven't had any direct contact," I explained, "but at one point I was in contact with one of her descendants. He helped me regrow Yggdrasil, at Hecate's behest, then disappeared soon after."

The waitress finally appeared at our tableside with a tray of drinks, setting down four glasses of water, one mug of coffee for me, and the open bottle of wine along with four glasses, though none of the rest of us intended on drinking. She gave me an odd look as she set the coffee in front of me, and I realized she'd probably caught a few words of our conversation. I just stared back at her. I'd gotten over my desire to keep up public appearances a long time ago.

With a final confused look, the waitress departed.

Loki poured himself a glass of wine, then asked, "So Hecate *wanted* you to regrow the tree, but has not ventured fully into this realm?" He took a sip of his wine, made a sour expression of distaste, then set his glass back on the table. "Perhaps she'd prefer you visit her instead."

"Come again?" I asked, wondering if he was truly suggesting what I thought he was suggesting.

"I think we've had our fill of traveling to different realms," Alaric interjected before Loki could answer.

"Agreed," Mikael muttered.

Loki smirked. "So you're just going to sit here and wait for the less benevolent gods to find you? Don't you want to know why you were truly created?"

"Of course," I replied, fiddling with my mug of coffee. "But I don't see how Hecate is going to help with that if *you* don't even know."

Loki tsked at me. "Foolish girl. If Hecate knew enough about you to help you regrow Yggdrasil, then I guarantee she knows more. You share the same energy, after all. She likely knows more about you than anyone else."

"But Mara—" I hesitated, "I mean the Morrigan, didn't know exactly how I came to be like this, and she and I were even closer in energy. The first time we tried to summon a goddess we got the Morrigan, not Hecate."

Loki rolled his eyes. "The Morrigan was practically a human woman. Hecate was never anything close to human. She's as old as time itself."

"So, say we do try to find her," Mikael cut in, "what does any of this matter to *you*?"

Loki smiled. "I have my reasons, reasons I have no intention of divulging. Regardless, the fact of the matter is that I'm the only one who can show you how to use Yggdrasil to locate Hecate's realm. You'll simply have to trust me."

"*Trust* the God of Lies?" Mikael asked skeptically.

I tensed. Loki might seem friendly enough, but it probably wasn't a good idea to insult him.

He raised an eyebrow at Mikael. "Whatever you say, child of Dolos. You expect the girl to trust *you*, do you not? Why am I any different?"

"Because I have proven myself," Mikael said boldly.

I didn't correct him. The fact of the matter was that Mikael *had* expected me to trust him right from the start, because I'd had no other choice. I didn't see much difference in the current situation.

Boots hissing across the low-pile carpeting preceded Sophie's arrival. Dressed in a sleek black dress with her long hair pulled back in a braid, she stood before us.

I watched as she assessed Loki's appearance, then said, "You don't look much like a god."

I sputtered on my coffee. I swear, being technically immortal can make people stupidly bold.

"I do *other* things like a god," Loki said lasciviously, waggling his eyebrows at her.

Sophie sighed, then gestured for Alaric to scoot over, which meant smushing me against the wall. We both acquiesced, and I was left barely able to move my elbows.

Before we could catch Sophie up on everything, the waitress returned with our food, placing my ravioli and garlic bread in front of me, and *five* other plates in front of Loki, including two desserts. He refilled his half-empty wine glass and peered down at his food with gluttonous eyes.

"Yeah," Sophie muttered, "*definitely* not a god."

Loki didn't seem to notice her comment as he began digging into his food.

"To catch you up," Alaric said to Sophie, "Loki is attempting to convince Madeline that she must venture into another realm to find Hecate in order to learn the purpose of her creation."

Sophie rolled her eyes, then swiped Loki's bottle of wine, filling the nearest clean glass for herself. She took a slow sip, then placed the glass on the table. "Well, I suppose it's not the *worst* idea I've ever heard. It's not as if we haven't traveled between realms before."

"You're a terrible influence," Mikael balked at her.

I watched as a smug smirk crossed her face. "Takes one to know one."

"I like her," Loki commented, his mouth half-full as he pushed away one empty plate to replace it with the next full one.

"Well I don't like you," Sophie sniped.

"Oh you will," Loki assured her, glancing up from his food. "Give me time."

I took a sip of my coffee and stared down at my meal, though my appetite had abruptly departed. I rubbed my free hand along my belly, thinking.

Could I trust Loki to take us to another realm? It was risky, but so was waiting around for the gods who might want to destroy me. I'd never met Hecate, but through Marcos, she had helped me once. She might just help me again.

I was starting to think it was a risk I might be willing to take, even if the thought of not only traveling to a different time, but to an entirely different realm, made me want to hide in bed and cry.

3

I stared up at the dark ceiling, too hot under the thick covers with Alaric's arm wrapped around my waist. We'd brought Loki home with us, passing him off as one of the Vaettir who'd flown in to join the clan. He'd willingly gone along with the ruse, and was now asleep in one of the guest rooms . . . or maybe he wasn't asleep, but I wasn't about to check on him.

I smoothed my hand along Alaric's bare arm, debating if I should wake him. He was an annoyingly heavy sleeper though, and probably wouldn't wake up regardless. I was on my own.

I gently pushed Alaric's arm off me, then crawled out of the covers and stood, thinking I'd move into the den to watch TV. I was a bit chilled in my black tank top and leggings as I tip-toed toward the door, then became distracted as something caught my eye out the open window, just a flash of white, but it seemed strange to me.

I approached the window, pushing the sheer white curtains aside to take a deep breath of rain-scented night air. I leaned forward and narrowed my eyes, peering out into the near darkness of the new moon.

There was *definitely* someone out there, standing still, peering back at me. I reached out with my senses, hoping to identify the form by its energy.

I gasped. Here we were just talking about Marcos, and he finally appears as if summoned.

I glanced over my shoulder at Alaric, still asleep on the bed, then crept out of the room. If Marcos was coming to us in the dead of night, I knew he'd want to speak to me alone.

Shutting the bedroom door gently behind me, I hurried down the dark hall toward one of the side doors leading out to the massive, forested yard. I let myself outside, enjoying the cool air on my too hot body. Soon enough my bare arms and leggings-clad legs had goose-bumps, and my bare feet were wet with the dew clinging to the grass.

Peering around in the darkness, I reached the place where I'd seen Marcos, though he was no longer there.

I stopped and looked around, narrowing my eyes to peer about the decorative shrubs, then the fir trees beyond.

"You have summoned a god," a male voice said directly behind me.

I jumped, then spun on him, taking in his long, pure white hair, and almost matching skin. He wore black, shapeless clothing. If I didn't know him, I would have thought him a ghost or some other creepy crawly, returned to the world along with other magics.

"Well, Mikael and Silver summoned him," I replied, "but yes. What are you doing here, Marcos?"

He tilted his head to the side, and I knew Hecate was whispering in his ear. After a moment, he explained, "My goddess bids you come and find her."

I narrowed my eyes at him. "Have you been spying on us?"

He pursed his thin lips. "Does it matter? My goddess has the answers you seek."

A shiver went up my spine. I might have had a hard time fully trusting Loki, but it was downright impossible to fully trust Marcos, though I'd been forced to do it in the past.

"Why can't *you* just give me the answers?" I asked.

He shook his head. "She requires you to come in person. She will not release her secrets easily, not even to *me*."

He seemed a little bitter about the last part, though I couldn't tell for sure. I rarely sensed any emotions from Marcos.

"So let me get this straight," I sighed. "Hecate wants me to drop everything and travel to her realm for answers, with no assurances that she even has what I need?"

He tilted his head again, listening, then explained, "She believes you are running out of time. Not only will the gods return, but other malevolent energies. They will be drawn to your light, and will be compelled to snuff it out."

I wrapped my arms around myself, suddenly cold. "What kind of malevolent energies? Many would have considered the banshees malevolent, but they weren't, not really."

Marcos glanced over his shoulder, then back to me. "I must leave you now, and you must make your choice. The god who has chosen you can show you the way there, though I advise he not enter Hecate's inner sanctum. She has a certain . . . *distaste* for the old gods."

I opened my mouth to say more, then someone hissed, "*Madeline!*"

I turned in the direction of the voice. It was Mikael. I glanced back at Marcos and cursed. He'd disappeared again, and finding him was unlikely.

I turned back to Mikael as he hurried toward me, dressed in an old fashioned burgundy night coat and pants, his feet bare like mine.

"What the hell are you doing out here with *him*?" he chastised, gesturing to where Marcos had stood.

"He wasn't going to hurt me," I sighed, rolling my eyes at his worried expression, "and we've been trying to find him for months. I wasn't going to just let him slip away before I could ask him about Hecate."

Mikael crossed his arms, trapping a lock of his russet hair, then sighed. "What did you find out?"

I shrugged. "Not much. Hecate wants me to come to her realm and find her, but Marcos warned me about Loki entering her inner sanctum. She has . . . *issues* with the old gods."

Mikael put an arm around my shoulders and guided me back toward the house. "We can discuss it further in the morning, if Loki is even still willing to take us."

I stopped, forcing him to stop beside me. "That reminds me, why were you so cranky about Loki coming instead of Dolos?"

He blinked down at me. "Seriously? We weren't trying to summon Dolos, we were trying to reach Silver's patron goddess, Veritas, the Goddess of Truth. We were trying to reach a peaceful goddess who would tell us only truths, and instead we received the god of mischief and chaos. We can't trust him as far as we can throw him."

I smirked, finally understanding his earlier attitude. "Speaking of trust, has Silver shown back up yet?"

Mikael chuckled. "No, and he likely won't as long as Loki is here. He was willing to face Veritas, but self-preservation has always been Silver's primary objective. He will not risk himself needlessly."

We started walking again, Mikael's arm still around my shoulders. "And you think working with Loki is a needless risk?" I questioned.

"For Silver perhaps," he replied, "but not for you. You

are already at great risk. I can grudgingly admit that gaining a god as an ally is a wise plan, even if it is Loki."

"And Hecate?" I questioned as we reached the door.

"*That*, we will discuss in the morning," he replied, opening it.

"But I can't sleep," I protested as we walked inside.

"Fine," he sighed. "One game of chess, then you're going to bed."

"Only if I lose," I argued. "If I win you have to play me again."

"You're impossible," he chuckled, shutting the door behind us.

He walked past me and led the way down the hall. I was about to play the best game of chess in my life, because there was no way I was going to be able to sleep that night.

I FINALLY MANAGED to go to sleep around three in the morning, so I was definitely not rested when Alaric awoke at six.

He gently stroked the side of my face, attempting to rouse me. "I really don't want Loki running around without supervision," he whispered.

"So go supervise," I groaned, clenching my eyes shut. "I've barely gotten any sleep."

He sighed, then stood. "Try not to sleep too long. We have much to consider today."

He quietly padded out of the room, shutting the door behind him.

I sat up with a huff, squinting at the sun coming in through the sheer curtains. I'd completely forgotten to tell Alaric about Marcos before he walked out. I wanted him to have all of the information before we discussed anything with Loki.

With a groan, I slipped out of bed then hurried into the bathroom.

I needed to find Alaric, but pregnancy bladder needed me more.

A few minutes later, I'd donned a robe over my tank top and black leggings, then left the room in search of Alaric. Knowing he'd want coffee, I headed toward the kitchen first.

On the way there, I passed through the den, where Alejandro sat on the sofa with Tallie, one of my favorites of our clan. Tallie's gray leggings and blue chunky sweater made her look even more petite than usual. Her sleek black hair was pulled up into a messy bun, accentuating her sharp cheekbones and delicate features.

She looked at me warily.

"Who's the new guy?" Alejandro asked from his seat beside her.

I cringed. They had to mean Loki. Tallie and Alejandro weren't from Mikael's original clan, so they wouldn't know about any characters from his past. "He helped Mikael a few years back," I lied, "and has come to join our clan. Be nice to him."

Alejandro nodded, readily accepting my answer, but Tallie still seemed wary. She was wary of everything though, and still seemed to be waiting for me to throw her out on the streets.

Unable to muster comforting words for someone else when I was in dire need of them myself, I walked past them to the adjoining hall near the front door and into the kitchen.

The blinds on the far wall were all open, showcasing an uncharacteristically sunny day. Behind the kitchen counter sat Loki and Sophie, but no Alaric.

Dressed in a fuzzy gray robe, Sophie sipped her coffee as she lifted her gaze toward me. "It's about time you woke up. I'm tired of babysitting duty."

"No one told you to babysit," I muttered, glancing past her toward the window, wondering where Alaric had gone.

I returned my gaze to her as she darted a glare toward Loki. "*You* told me you were supposed to be watched at all times."

He shrugged. "It was the only excuse I could think of to compel you to spend time with me."

I sighed heavily, then walked to the coffee pot and poured myself a cup. "Have either of you seen Alaric?"

"I think he's outside," Sophie muttered, her glare still on Loki.

With my steamy cup filled and creamer added, I walked around the counter and past them toward the French double doors leading from the kitchen to the yard. I opened one clear window-paneled door and stepped outside, knowing Sophie would continue to *watch* Loki even after his trick. The Vaettir did not trust easily, especially when it came to the old gods.

Soothed by the crisp morning air, I padded barefoot across the wood porch that dominated this side of the house toward where I'd spotted Alaric, already dressed in his usual black jeans and tee-shirt, gazing out at the fir trees as he sipped his coffee.

I reached his side. "Sorry, I was half asleep when you left. There's a lot I want to catch you up on before we make a decision."

"Mikael already told me," he explained, gesturing as the statuesque Viking came into view from around the back side of the house. They'd clearly been having a morning conversation without me.

"My apologies," Mikael said as he reached us. "Nature called."

Ugh, why were men always peeing outside, even at home? He wore an outfit similar to Loki's, a lightweight tunic over suede pants. He dressed more modern when we went to town, but at home, he liked his comforts.

Alaric seemed annoyed, but didn't say anything. I took his free hand in mine, wondering if he was annoyed with me, and got a limp squeeze in return. *Yep*, definitely annoyed with me.

"Don't give me a hard time," I grumbled. "It's not like I invited Marcos here. He came to see me."

He sighed. "Please don't empath me, Madeline."

39

Irritated, I pulled my hand away from his, sipped my coffee, then replied, "I don't need to be an empath to know you're annoyed."

He sighed. "You should have woken me. Marcos could have been here to kidnap you, or worse."

"I can handle Marcos," I muttered.

Mikael watched us cautiously, clearly not wanting to get in the middle of our bickering.

The French doors opened behind us, and Loki and Sophie emerged.

"Have we reached a decision?" Loki inquired. "Shall we venture into Hecate's realm?"

"*No*," Alaric answered, while I said, "Yes."

He turned his hurt gaze to me.

"We don't have a choice," I argued with that silent, accusing gaze. Part of me wished we could have just stayed in bed this morning with him in a good mood, no arguments necessary, but we *did* need to move forward.

"Madeline," he began patiently. "I've been trapped in other realms *twice* since I met you. I'd really not like to be trapped a third."

I crossed my arms, suddenly angry, though I knew at the root of my ire was fear. I didn't want to get trapped in another realm either, especially with my daughter on the way.

I shifted my gaze past Alaric to Mikael, standing a few paces back. "Isn't there some sort of oath we can make him take?" I nodded toward Loki. "Something that ensures he has to bring us back in one piece?"

Loki lifted his hand in the air, palm facing outward. "I hereby solemnly swear that I will try my absolute best to return you to this realm in one piece."

Sophie scowled. "That's somehow not reassuring."

He turned his head toward her, trailing a lock of vibrant red hair over his shoulder. "Would you like me to sign a contract in blood?"

"That's actually not a bad idea," I mused. I turned toward Mikael. "Can blood oaths be made between the Vaettir and gods?"

I'd used a blood oath to ensure Mikael wouldn't betray us when we'd first formed a partnership. The ritual had made me a bit uneasy, but in the end, I'd felt a lot better knowing that if he broke his oath, the earth would *claim* him.

"Ye-ah," Loki said, drawing out the word. "I'm not really into creating blood oaths with big angry death balls."

"What if I say it's the only way we're going?" I pressed, taking a step toward him. Alaric had crossed his arms to peer out at the trees, ignoring us.

Loki scowled. "Then I'd say we're not going. I have no intention of betraying you, but I like to keep my options open."

I crossed my arms, keeping one hand slightly extended with my coffee cup. "Well you're going to have to offer us *some* sort of assurance."

Everyone, including Alaric, turned to watch him as

he thought things over. He snapped his fingers as an idea came to him.

He lifted one finger into the air. "I can offer you the best assurance of all. Since you're pure energy in a mortal shell, more akin to gods than humans, I believe I can teach you how to travel the branches of Yggdrasil yourself. I will not be able to trap you in another realm, because you will be able to return on your own."

I looked to Alaric and Mikael, wondering if what Loki claimed could be true.

Mikael stroked his chin in thought. "It's sound in theory, as long as Madeline feels sure she'll be able to manage the World Tree herself *before* we go anywhere."

Loki held out his hand to me. "I believe we have a deal."

I glanced at Alaric, who was clearly still upset, but wasn't stopping me, then stepped toward Loki and took his hand.

We shook on it, and the pact was made. I was going to learn how to travel to other realms using Yggdrasil. I'd used the tree for time travel once before, but this was far more exciting . . . or maybe it was just terrifying. I hadn't quite decided.

4

An hour later, having agreed to learn how to travel through Yggdrasil, I was strapped in the backseat of one of the two vehicles that headed toward the beach. Next to me was Alaric, our backpacks in the middle. We each had a change of clothes, a winter coat, and enough food and water to last for days. I'd dressed in heavy-weight jeans with a belly band, a loose green flannel, and hiking boots, since we weren't quite sure what sort of biome we'd be entering, and we had no idea how far we'd need to hike to find Hecate. I had twin daggers ready to affix to my belt once we reached the beach, and two more already hidden at my ankles. While some of the other Vaettir would be bringing swords and axes, I was far more comfortable with the smaller weapons.

Aila, Mikeal's tall, blonde, and deadly second in command drove, and Loki rode in the passenger seat. The other vehicle held Faas, Mikael, Frode, Sophie, and

Alejandro. Everyone in the vehicles had now been informed of our plan, and of Loki's true identity, but we'd be telling no one else. Things might get out of hand if the clan knew both their Doyens were in another realm. Aila and Alejandro would be remaining behind to watch the clan, but had accompanied us since we needed someone to drive the vehicles home in case we were gone overnight. Faas and Frode would be coming into the other world with us. Faas, because he understood *energy* better than any of us, and Frode for extra muscle, just in case.

Alaric took my hand and gave it a squeeze. "You know I'm only upset because I'm worried," he muttered.

I nodded. "I know, and I'm sorry. I'm the reason we never seem able to live in peace."

"You're also the reason we're free from Estus and the key. Do not apologize."

I squeezed his hand, feeling better. The situation was already dire, and I really hated adding a lover's spat to the mix.

"How sweet," Loki commented, watching us in the rearview mirror. "I had no idea death energy could be so *loving.*"

"I'm more than just death energy," I grumbled.

Maybe that was why Hecate disliked the old gods. She got tired of being called a death goddess all the time, when she was so much more. Although, I supposed Loki probably got called a lot of names too.

The trees thinned as we neared the coast. The silver

car containing our friends turned off the highway ahead of us, taking the same narrow road Alaric and I had taken the previous day.

I let out a long breath, then gently removed my hand from Alaric's to make sure I had everything I needed in my pack. I switched off my cell phone and stuffed it back into an exterior pocket of the pack. It wouldn't work in another realm, but I wanted to make sure we'd be able to call Aila and Alejandro to pick us up when we returned.

Yggdrasil came into view as we made our way down the bumpy, narrow dirt road, its golden branches vibrant in the harsh sun. The silver car parked ahead of us, and Aila maneuvered the truck into the narrow space beside it.

We all exited the vehicles, hoisting our packs onto our backs and affixing weapons that had been too awkward to wear while crammed in the vehicles.

Loki sauntered toward the tree line unhindered, having refused a backpack or any other supplies. He didn't seem to mind that he was weaponless and still in the same outfit we'd found him in.

Alaric came around the side of the vehicle to stand near me. "Are you entirely sure about this?" he asked softly.

I nodded. "As long as I feel confident that I can bring us back without Loki's help, it will be fine."

As Mikael wordlessly led the way down toward the beach, Alejandro fell into step at my other side. He flipped his dark hair over his shoulder then flashed me a smile. "If you don't come back, can I have your truck?"

I rolled my eyes at him, then aimed them downward, watching my footing as I carefully picked my way toward the beach through the brambles bordering the forest. "If you touch my truck, I'll haunt you from the other side."

He pouted. "Aw, you're no fun."

I laughed, then turned away. Alaric took my hand. I glanced at him to see his gaze on the distant World Tree.

"I hope we don't have to physically climb it," I commented.

He smiled. "Don't worry. All you'd have to do is climb on my back."

I chuckled, taking comfort in his presence. Loki might leave us all for dead, but Alaric and Mikael would both stand by me to the bitter end.

Loki reached the tree first, shortly followed by Aila and Mikael, basically those with the longest legs. As we followed their footprints in the sand, Faas walked silently behind me, but I could sense his nerves.

I released Alaric's hand from my grip as we reached the tree. Up close, it looked more silver than gold, at least in the areas the sun didn't hit.

"Time for your lesson," Loki instructed, stretching his hand toward me.

I glanced nervously at Alaric, then stepped forward.

Loki gently grasped my wrist, guiding my palm against the tree. "Do you feel that?"

I closed my eyes, focusing on the impossibly smooth

bark beneath my palm. The tree was formed of the fates, the key's chaos energy, and the Morrigan's emotion and life/death energy. They were all highly familiar to me. Almost comforting.

"I can feel Mara's energy," I said softly, then opened my eyes to look at him. "I mean the Morrigan."

He nodded. "Good. That you are familiar with the energy should prove useful. It is not difficult to travel through the tree. The difficult part is ending up in the right place."

I frowned, thinking about the countless realms to where the branches might lead. We could end up *anywhere*.

"Fortunately," Loki continued, "you've come in contact with Hecate's energy signature before."

I tensed, thinking he'd somehow found out about my meeting with Marcos, then relaxed, remembering that I'd explained to him how Hecate had helped guide me to regrow the tree, if only in a small way.

He pressed his hand over mine, making a firm connection with the tree. "All you need do is tune in to the tree's energy, then focus on the energy signature you would like to reach. That was how I ended up here. I was examining one of the branches, and I sensed you on the other side. I focused on your energy, and *poof!*"

"Sounds simple enough," I commented.

"Not simple at all," he countered, "but still, easily done for beings like you and I."

Still pressing my palm against the tree, he gestured

47

for everyone to gather round. As everyone moved in, he explained, "You will be the one to take us to Hecate. In doing so, I will have upheld my end of the bargain. You will have proven you can travel the tree without my magic."

I glanced at Faas as he moved to my other side. "I'll watch him to make sure it is only your power transporting us."

I nodded. "Thanks."

As everyone gathered even closer, Mikael said a few words to Aila and Alejandro before they stepped away.

"You might want to go farther back than that," Loki called out to the pair, who'd only taken a few steps before turning to watch us. "As this is her first time, she might accidentally sweep you up." He turned back to me. "Now Madeline, focus on the tree's energy."

As Aila and Alejandro jogged away, I did as he asked, which wasn't difficult. My eyes fluttered closed, and my muscles slowly relaxed as I fell into the familiar rhythm of the tree's energy. Slowly, my awareness expanded. I could feel the tree's shimmering roots reaching deep into the sand, and the impossibly high branches kissing the sky.

I became so enraptured that I almost didn't hear Loki as he said, "Now focus on Hecate's energy, focus on her name, for names hold power. Use Yggdrasil's magic to bring us to her realm."

Since I'd never met Hecate personally, I focused on the feel of Marcos' magic. Not on Marcos' himself, but the taste and power of true necromancy in its most potent form. Hecate.

I had a feeling of weightlessness as my surroundings seemed to slip away. For a moment I became frightened. It felt almost as if I no longer had a body, and I feared for the tiny life growing inside me.

Then my hiking boots touched down on loamy soil. I stumbled to the side, dizzy. Two set of hands reached out and caught me.

I opened my eyes to see both Alaric and Faas holding on to me, watching me as if I might faint. I glanced up toward a golden branch dangling overhead, as if the tree it belonged to was rooted in the sky, growing down toward the earth rather than up.

"I'm fine," I muttered, and they slowly released me as I stepped away.

We were in a dense forest, *no,* not quite a forest, more like a jungle. The trees around us seemed vaguely tropical, but at the same time the soil was dark instead of sandy. The damp air was pleasantly warm on my skin.

Loki peered around as he walked toward me. "Well," he began, "the ride wasn't exactly smooth, but congratulations on getting us here. I honestly assumed it would take more than one try."

"So we made it?" I questioned in disbelief. "We made it to Hecate's realm?"

"Yes," Loki replied.

Faas let out a gasp. "And we lost our magic in the process."

We all whirled on him.

Pushing his long blond bangs away from his face, he lifted his pale, horrified eyes up to meet mine.

"I can't feel anyone's energy," he explained.

I tilted my head, confused. I could still feel the pulse of my magic beneath my skin, amplified from our trip through Yggdrasil's branches.

I turned my attention to Frode. "Try freezing something," I instructed.

Turning his broad back away from us, he lifted his hands, but nothing happened. Normally he could summon ice with his magic.

I shook my head. "I don't understand. I can still feel my magic."

Faas *harrumphed* in irritation. "We are such fools. Of course we don't have magic here. We are not a part of this realm. Our magic is tied to *our* realm."

"Then why do I still have magic?" I questioned.

Loki scowled. "I do not have my magic either. Hecate must have nullified all magical signatures in this realm except her own. You still have magic, because you share similar energy. You truly are cut from goddess cloth, pure transcendental energy."

"Well if we didn't have proof of that theory before . . . " Mikael trailed off. He paced around the small clearing, hand on the axe at his belt. Not his father's axe, I realized, wondering if he feared he might lose it in another realm.

Alaric put an arm around my waist and pulled me

backwards. "There's something out there," he whispered, his lips pressed against my ear.

I tensed. I still had my magic, and everyone was physically armed. We could probably handle whatever was out there . . . unless it was Hecate.

I darted my gaze from tree to tree, but could not yet see what Mikael and Alaric had sensed. Everyone else gathered close around us while Mikael and Loki investigated.

Alaric whirled me around as something rustled in the bushes behind us.

"Halt!" a woman's voice demanded.

I watched as she stepped out of her hiding place, followed by several other women. They all held massive, gleaming steel spears, aimed in our direction. The finely made spears seemed out of place with their flowing white dresses, cinched at their waists with thin brown belts. Most had hair down to their waists in varying colors, with some tresses pulled back in loose braids.

"Hecate's handmaidens," Loki commented, suddenly standing right beside me.

Noticing Loki, the women began to mutter amongst themselves, then the first one who'd spoken, a brunette who couldn't have been more than twenty, called out, "You are not welcome here, old god!"

"Do you think they're talking to me?" Loki asked facetiously, then snickered.

"We're here to see Hecate," Mikael explained, stepping out ahead of the group while Loki stayed back with us.

The woman in the lead shifted her feet, then muttered something to her comrades I couldn't quite hear.

"They know who you are," Alaric whispered in my ear.

"So you still have your acute hearing?" I asked softly.

"That is part of my physiology," he explained, "not my magic."

"We will bring the woman to Hecate," the brunette explained. "The old god must stay behind."

I looked to Loki, who shrugged.

That was all fine and well for him, but I didn't want to venture into a goddess' inner sanctum with only *my* magic. If the others still had their abilities, I might be willing to leave Loki behind, but I didn't trust my magic enough to protect everyone on my own.

"He comes, or we leave right now," I decided. "Hecate asked me to come to her, now she's going to have to meet me halfway."

The women muttered amongst themselves again, then turned back to us. "You and a single escort will come to the border, the others may follow behind," she ordered. "Hecate will meet you there."

I hadn't meant for Hecate to literally meet me halfway, but I supposed I was getting what I wanted, so I kept my mouth shut.

The women turned to lead the way, leaving us little choice but to follow.

"Walk with Mikael," Alaric instructed quietly. "If any negotiations are needed, he will be the one of most use to you."

I peered at him for a moment, then nodded. Mikael was the most skilled negotiator among us. It made sense for him to stay at my side.

Having heard his name, he approached and offered me his arm. "I'd be honored to face the goddess with you."

I hoisted my pack more securely on my back, then placed my arm in Mikael's. I gave Alaric a final worried look, then started forward. Everyone else brought up the rear, talking amongst themselves in low voices.

The women led us down a well-trod path through the foliage. Now that I had time to really observe our surroundings, I noticed strange, brightly colored songbirds up in the trees. Their lilting melodies were so beautiful, I could hardly believe they were real. The further we traveled down the path, the more vibrant flowers there were spread amongst the odd, tropical trees, producing an almost overwhelming scent.

At this point it felt as if we'd crossed some sort of magical barrier, right where the flowers had increased. I glanced back to make sure everyone was still behind us. Alaric, walking beside Sophie, nodded at me encouragingly.

I turned my attention forward as white tents came

into view in the distance. I had a feeling we were about to reach the edge of Hecate's inner sanctum. I wondered if Yggdrasil's branch being so close to it was merely coincidental, or if Hecate had intentionally set up shop in the vicinity. Now that we were so near, I felt a little silly for wearing hiking boots and a camp pack to meet a goddess.

While most of the women walking ahead of us continued onward, the brunette turned back to face us, leaning casually against her spear. "You will wait here," she ordered.

Ready for a rest, even after such a short walk, I pulled my arm from Mikael's and slipped my pack from my shoulders, leaning it against a nearby tree. I almost considered sitting, but I really didn't want everyone to see me awkwardly climbing back to my feet when Hecate arrived. Being pregnant amongst perfectly fit people is the pits.

I glanced behind us as Sophie and the others lowered their packs to the ground, not understanding why they all had to stay behind. If Hecate wanted them out of earshot, she had another thing coming. Alaric and Sophie at least could still hear us from this distance.

I glanced in the other direction as the brunette turned toward some of the other women appearing behind her. They flocked around a tall woman with long auburn hair.

I knew the instant I saw her that the auburn-haired woman was Hecate. Though she appeared just an inch or two shorter than my 5'9", she seemed almost frail, but carried herself with a quiet dignity. Her dress was similar to what her handmaidens wore, except the fabric seemed to be spun from pure gold. It glistened in the gentle sunlight filtering down through the broad leaves of the nearby trees.

She stopped roughly twenty feet away from us. I had to rub my eyes to clear them as I watched the foliage around her, but even after blinking several times, the plants still seemed to move. As I watched, several flowers near her feet bloomed.

"Welcome, Madeline!" she called out.

I shivered as she said my name. She was what I had pictured a goddess looking like, somehow much more impressive than Loki, though perhaps it was all a show for our benefit.

Mikael took my arm again as Hecate swayed toward us, a mischievous smile curling her pink lips. She looked me up and down, then turned her gaze to Mikael. Her delicate nose sniffed the air. "You are practically mortal," she said with distaste.

"Only in this realm," Mikael assured.

Hecate nodded. "One escort for Madeline, that is all."

I chewed my lip, then turned to look over my shoulder at Alaric, standing with the others well out of reach.

He shrugged, which was uncharacteristic for him. Why wasn't he worried? Something was off.

"What's going on?" I asked, turning back toward Hecate.

She frowned. "I wish to negotiate. You and I are the same. I would never harm you. Step forward with your chosen escort and I will tell you everything you wish to know. The others will not be harmed."

I looked to Alaric again. He nodded.

I turned my attention to Mikael.

He patted my hand where it rested on his arm. "I will accept the role of escort."

We all turned to Loki.

He raised his hands in surrender. "Hey, I'm just here to watch anyways."

Mikael took my arm and guided me forward as Hecate turned to walk beside us. We kept walking until we were at the spot where the flowers had bloomed at her feet. I felt an odd twinge of magic, like we'd passed another barrier. I wasn't sure if Hecate was aware that some of the Vaettir, like Alaric and Sophie, would still be able to hear her from this distance, even if she whispered, but I wasn't about to let her in on that secret.

"Madeline," she sighed softly, seeming relieved that I was now close to her, surrounded by her handmaidens. Her entire demeanor seemed to shift. Suddenly she seemed like the most kindly grandmother, trapped in a younger woman's body. "I'm so glad you were able to come," she whispered. Darting her gaze past us, she added, "Even if you brought one of the old gods into my realm."

She turned her sparkling green gaze back to me. "You have already achieved so much," she said softly. "I knew you had the ability to regrow Yggdrasil, but to actually follow through? You were willing to sacrifice *everything*, and I would expect no less."

I wasn't quite sure what to say to her. She was suddenly acting like I was her best friend in the world.

"So," I hesitated, "about why you brought me here . . . "

"Oh yes," she continued. "I want you to stay here where you and your child will be safe. I will return to your world in your place and set things right."

I stared at her. "Why can't you just come back to my realm *with* me? I mean, I'd appreciate your help, but I can't stay here."

Rage washed across her expression, then was gone. It had been so brief that I almost would have questioned if I'd seen it at all. That was, if I couldn't still sense her emotions. Her anger was like fire ants marching up my skin.

I glanced at Mikael, wishing I could tell him what I was sensing.

Hecate sighed. "I cannot go into that world while you are there. If we are in a single place together, the energy that fuels us is shared. I need all of my power if I am to face the old gods."

"So you're saying you and I are sharing our power here?" I questioned.

She chuckled. "No no, Madeline. This is *my* realm,

created especially for me. You cannot best me here, if that's what you're thinking."

I *was* thinking it, but I shook my head. "Not at all," I lied. "I just don't quite understand. You said you'd tell me why I was created."

She tilted her head. "You truly do not know, do you?"

I wanted to yell at her in frustration, but I bit my tongue. "I have no way of knowing," I said honestly.

She sighed, then smiled. "Alright, I'll explain it to you. You were created when the Morrigan perished, she was created when the World Tree was torn asunder."

"Um, no," I replied. "I'm not that old."

She tsked at me. "Of course not. You've died and been reborn many times. You are only the latest incarnation of my energy. You were not created by any one individual, you simply *are*. Your energy must exist in the world, and so it has perpetuated."

"So, I was *born* like a normal person?" I asked.

She chuckled. "Of course. *Everyone* is born, except perhaps the Morrigan. She was spontaneously created, but everyone *else* is born."

"Fancy that," I commented. "So if I'm meant to be in the world, why would the old gods want to destroy me?"

"The old gods do not understand you and I," she said conspiratorially. "We are a pure part of nature. *They* are merely elevated humans."

I glanced at Mikael, who seemed to be deep in thought, not offering me any help.

I turned back to her. "While I appreciate the information. I'm not sure how it helps my situation."

"I already told you," she chided. "You will stay here where you and your child are safe. I will even permit your consort to remain with you. *I* will return to your realm and solve all of your problems."

"I'm sorry," I replied. "I can't do that. Too many people are depending on me." I gestured to Mikael. "On *us*. We are Doyens of a clan."

Hecate simply smiled.

"Step back, Madeline," Mikael ordered, as if noticing something I hadn't. He put a hand on my shoulder and pulled me out of Hecate's reach.

I suddenly noticed that it was eerily quiet behind us. I turned to find that everyone was *gone*, including Hecate's handmaidens.

"They were never with us," Mikael hissed. "It was an illusion. They are likely back where we landed with the handmaidens."

"Oh no," Hecate purred. "They followed you for a time, but were led down a different path when you crossed the first of my barriers."

"I don't understand!" I cried, glancing frantically around for Alaric, and for everyone else.

"She tricked us," Mikael explained, tugging me further back.

"B-but why?" I asked, directing my gaze toward Hecate. "Why negotiate for us to step forward, if no one else was even there at all?"

Hecate chuckled. "You had to enter the second barrier of my realm willingly for my spell to work. I had to get you this far, by allowing you to think you were in control."

I took another step backward, and it was like I'd hit a wall. "What did you do to them?" I growled, flattening my palms against the invisible barrier.

I felt sick and dizzy, but if this woman had done something to Alaric and the others, I would tear her heart out, goddess or no.

"They will be returned to your realm," she explained. "Do not fear, they are safe. You and I are friends, even if you don't realize it now."

I glanced at Mikael, then back to her. "Is he *real*?" I asked.

"Of course I'm real!" he replied.

Hecate nodded. "I told you I would not deprive you of your consort. I did not lie. He will remain here, safe with you and your growing child."

I whipped my gaze to Mikael, eyes wide.

He eyed me intently, silently urging me not to blow his cover.

I took a deep breath. He was right. I wasn't about to let her know he wasn't my consort and have him taken away too. There was one thing I didn't understand though. Marcos knew Alaric was the father of my child. Why had he not told Hecate? Didn't he tell her *everything*?

"Come now," she instructed happily. "I will show you to your lodgings."

"I don't think so," I replied, backing against the invisible wall once more. We just needed to get back to Yggdrasil's branch and we could return to our world.

Several handmaidens appeared behind Hecate and started toward us.

Mikael moved to my side and took my hand. "Do not fight just yet," he whispered. "We will escape when the time is right."

I nodded, though I was struggling to fight back tears. I *couldn't* be trapped in this realm. I needed to go home, even if it meant I had to face every single one of the old gods. Any fate was better than being trapped here.

The handmaidens closed in around us, grabbing our arms, and guiding us forward.

Hecate turned and walked ahead of us toward the distant white tents. I watched her narrow back and felt nothing but rage. I had a new number one enemy on my list. It could be a long list at times, but I never forgot any of the names.

5

Alaric lifted a hand to his head. Someone was squirming beneath him. He pushed away from the second body as his vision slowly returned. Damp sand soaked into his pants.

"Damn it," he cursed under his breath, looking up at the golden tree before him.

"My sentiments exactly," Faas muttered behind him, seeming relieved to no longer be crushed by Alaric's weight.

"Where the hell is Loki?" Sophie's voice growled.

Alaric glanced over his shoulder. A few paces behind Faas, Frode was helping Sophie stand. Loki, Madeline, and Mikael were nowhere to be seen.

He pinched the bridge of his nose to stave off his headache, then looked back up at the tree. They'd been following behind Madeline and Mikael toward Hecate. He hadn't liked the idea, but as long as Madeline was within sight, he would be able to rush to her rescue. Then suddenly they'd hit an invisible wall. The next thing he remembered was landing rather harshly on this blasted beach, without Madeline, as if they'd been thrown away.

He struggled to his feet, then stumbled toward Yggdrasil, running his palms across the smooth bark. There had to be some way to go back to Madeline. He realized now that Hecate had tricked them. She'd lured Madeline to her realm, then sent the rest of them back to theirs . . . but then, where were Mikael and Loki? Mikael might be imprisoned with Madeline, but Loki?

He concentrated on the tree, though he knew it was futile. He did not possess the power to return to Hecate's realm. He could only pray that Hecate did not intend to harm Madeline.

A hand alighted on his shoulder, and he turned to see Sophie's worried expression.

"We were fools to ever trust Loki," he muttered.

She nodded. "Yes, we were, but," she aimed her gaze upward toward Yggdrasil's branches, "there are more gods where he came from. Gods that can bring us back to Hecate's realm."

He cupped his hand over hers, yet lingering on his shoulder. "Thank you for understanding. We have to go back, no matter what it takes."

Sophie nodded, her hand slipping back to her side, just as Faas approached. "I don't think Loki did this," he explained, flicking his sand-speckled blond hair out of his face. "I think he was caught up in the illusion just like we were."

"So where is he?" Sophie asked.

Faas shook his head. "Perhaps imprisoned, just like Madeline, and I assume Mikael too."

"But why Mikael?" Sophie questioned.

Frode walked toward them, brushing damp sand from his jeans. Joining the group, he said, "The why is not important. What's important is our clan is now missing both of its Doyens."

"That's not important," Alaric growled. "What's important is getting Madeline back."

Frode frowned. "So summon your goddess. The two of you are descended from Bastet, are you not? Ask her to aid you."

"Bastet is a goddess of war," Sophie replied. "I do not foresee her wanting to aid us."

Frode raised a blond eyebrow at her. "Do you want Madeline back, or not?"

Damn it, Alaric thought. He was right. He gazed back up to the tree. It had taken Madeline to gain Loki's attention, what would it take to call down another one of the gods? Not to mention, they didn't even know how to deal with Hecate. She might just send them back again, godless.

He looked to his sister. "We need to figure out what Hecate plans. We need to find Marcos."

"But how?" she questioned, her dark eyes wide.

He turned to Faas. "You can track energy, can

you not?"

He nodded. "Yes, but not as well as Tallie."

"Marcos was at the house last night," he explained, divulging the information that had previously been kept between him, Madeline, and Mikael.

"And you let him escape!" Sophie exclaimed.

Alaric glared at her. "*I* did not see him." He turned back to Faas. "Do you think you can track him?"

He nodded. "If he has remained in the area, yes."

Alaric looked back up to the tree, the only gateway to Marcos' goddess. "I highly doubt he's gone far," he muttered, "and at this point, he is our only link to Madeline."

"Alaric!" a voice shouted in a strong Scandinavian accent.

He turned to see Aila running toward them down the beach, her bright blonde ponytail streaming behind her. Soon enough she reached them and hunched over, panting heavily, not from exhaustion, he realized, but from panic.

"What are you doing here?" he questioned.

She straightened. "I have come in hopes Mikael would return soon. Magic is running amok. We believe the old gods have arrived, and there will be hell to pay."

Alaric's eyes widened, then slid toward Sophie. The old gods returning meant only one thing to him in that moment. A way to reach Madeline.

❄

"THIS IS BAD," I groaned.

"We're still alive, Madeline," Mikael replied, aiming his amber eyes at me.

I leaned back against the colorful cushions in the outdoor, harem style space . . . the harem style space surrounded by iron bars and handmaidens with spears. The roof of our outdoor cell shaded us from the dwindling sun, and thick carpets laid across the raw earth provided a surface for the ornate, colorful cushions.

Mikael's eyes met mine for a moment, then flicked to the handmaidens. We needed to be careful what we said.

Hecate had left shortly after imprisoning us. I wanted to fight, but Mikael had held me at bay. At the time, I'd thought he was right. The time to escape would be after Hecate left us, but now she had, and we were in an oddly lavish prison with no way out. I still had my magic, but bursts of energy wouldn't do much good against solid metal bars.

I rolled my eyes back to Mikael. It was beginning to grow dark, and I *really* did not want to spend the night in our prison.

"Come here," Mikael requested, holding out his arm as he leaned back on the cushions across from me.

I narrowed my eyes in suspicion. If he was about to flirt with me *now*, I was going to punch him.

He beckoned me with his hand, his expression saying, *don't argue, just get the hell over here.*

I sighed, stood and waddled over to him, then slumped back down onto the cushions beside him.

His arm, inches from mine, shifted minutely, drawing my attention down. There was a single thin dagger, more like a letter opener, in his hand, hidden between the cushions. They'd taken all of our other weapons, but he'd somehow smuggled it through.

I sighed. A dagger wasn't going to do us much good against multiple armed handmaidens. They'd easily confiscated all our other weapons.

Mikael angled his gaze toward the barred door of our outdoor cell, and the heavy padlock keeping it closed. I could see a set of keys dangling from the belts of each of the handmaiden guards.

Suddenly the dagger made sense. If the guard detail lowered at any point, we could probably lure one against the bars, place the blade at her throat, and steal her keys.

Now we just had to get rid of some guards.

"Night will come soon," Mikael said cryptically. "It will be time for rest."

I nodded. It was our best bet. We'd simply have to wait for the right opportunity.

ALARIC PEERED out the passenger seat window as Aila drove them down the highway. In the back seat Sophie, Faas, and Frode sat in silence

He could see flashes of color and lights in the slowly darkening woods surrounding the highway. The return of magic had clearly increased, but was it truly the old gods, or simply beings of other realms who'd discovered Yggdrasil's newly grown branches?

While he'd been dreading the old gods' return, now he hoped for it. Hecate had proven herself their true enemy, and Loki himself had said he wasn't the only god who didn't want to destroy Madeline.

"Has anything been on the news?" he questioned distantly, keeping his eyes on the passing trees.

"That's how we first realized something had changed," Aila explained. "Alejandro and I reached the house to find everyone in a panic. Hillsboro is experiencing massive blackouts, and there have been countless car accidents whose victims are claiming they saw spectral forms in the road."

He clenched his fists. Could this be a result of them using the World Tree to reach Hecate, or had this increased magical . . . *leakage* been inevitable? Or, was this all Hecate's doing? Had she taken Maddy away only to enter their realm herself?

"Our first priority is still to find Marcos," he decided. "We must learn what Hecate is planning."

Aila turned off the highway onto the road toward the house. "We'll recruit a few others along with Faas and Tallie to track him, then send another group into Hillsboro to see what's really going on."

He gripped his knees, unable to quiet his anxiety. Did Aila have to drive so slowly down the neighborhood road? "Yes," he agreed. "Do what you need in Hillsboro. I must focus on Madeline."

Aila glanced at him as she drove, then turned her eyes back to the road. Finally, they reached the last turnoff that would lead to their long, winding driveway.

"I hate to be the one to bring this up," Sophie began from the back seat, "but what are we going to do with Marcos once we find him? He's a powerful necromancer. He might have spent the past months gathering power. How will we make him talk?"

They hit the driveway and started down while Alaric mulled over Sophie's question. Madeline had been the one to keep Marcos in line before. If he was able to gather enough energy, he was a force to be reckoned with.

"Who is that?" Aila asked, narrowing her eyes as they neared the end of the dark drive.

Alaric looked toward the house. The headlights illuminated a woman walking around outside, glancing at her surroundings as if confused. Her long, flaxen hair glistened in the artificial light, draped over an icy lavender tunic and black pants.

Aila parked the vehicle a few feet from the woman, who'd turned to gaze at them with pale eyes.

"Um," Sophie began, leaning forward in her seat to place herself between Alaric and Aila, "correct me if I'm wrong, but isn't that woman dressed a bit like Loki?"

"Another of the old gods?" Aila asked.

Alaric threw open his door and hurried out of the car.

The woman watched him approach, hands on hips,

then looked past him to the others.

"Ah," the woman observed, "there you are." She walked around Alaric as if he didn't exist.

He turned to see her stop in front of Aila, who blinked at her in disbelief. "Freyja?" she questioned breathily.

Alaric stared at the woman's back. The *goddess'* back. It had to be true since she'd recognized her descendant, Aila, almost instantly.

Faas, Sophie, and Frode kept their distance, seemingly unsure of the new goddess.

"What are you doing here?" Aila questioned, clearly still astonished. "Have all of the gods returned?"

Freyja snorted. "Hardly. We had all agreed to bide our time until it was clear Yggdrasil was stable, then Loki hopped down a branch when no one was looking. I'm here to find him and bring him back."

Alaric gave Freyja a wide berth as he moved to stand beside Aila. Aila glanced at him, clearly asking permission to tell Freyja the truth.

Not wanting her to divulge that some of them had used Yggdrasil themselves, he turned to Freyja and explained, "He was here for a time, but now we don't know where he went, nor why he left."

Freyja rolled her eyes. "*Of course* I missed him, that blasted gnat." She glanced back at the house, then to Aila. "Is this your abode? I could stand a meal before I continue my search."

"Of course!" Aila replied, more flustered than Alaric

had ever seen her. She gestured for Freyja to lead the way toward the door.

With a nod, Freyja turned and sauntered onward with Aila hurrying after her.

Alaric hung back with the others until Freyja and Aila had entered the house, shutting the door behind them.

"I do not think we should divulge anything about Hecate until we can find Marcos and learn her plan," he explained, keeping his voice low as he eyed the closed door.

He turned to see the others nod their agreement.

"I'll go around the yard and see if I can pick up his energy signature," Faas whispered.

"I'll find Tallie and quietly bring her out," Frode added.

Alaric met Sophie's gaze, nodded, then turned back to Frode and Faas. "Sophie and I will see what we can learn from our newly acquired goddess."

Alaric turned to lead the way toward the house while Faas branched off toward the side yard.

He felt a small sliver of hope blooming within his chest. If they learned they could trust Freyja, she could take them back through the World Tree to find Madeline.

He'd have to be quite sure though that Freyja had no ill intentions toward Madeline. If she did, he'd need to come to terms with the fact that Maddy was likely better off lost . . . at least for the time being.

6

The sky had grown dark, and the guard duty still hadn't thinned. Two women in flowing white dresses, cinched at the waist with leather belts, guarded the barred door of our strange, outdoor cell, and four more were placed around the perimeter.

Mikael and I had bided our time, but there really hadn't been much to do besides eat the dinners we were brought and stare out at the lush jungle beginning roughly fifty feet from our cell.

It seemed the handmaiden guards all lived in small white tents, unless there were structures on the far side of the sanctum that I couldn't see.

I yawned, then shifted uncomfortably on my cushion. I *really* had to pee, but I didn't want to ask to go until the timing was right. A bathroom break would likely be our best bet of escaping, whereupon we could hopefully confiscate the cell door keys.

I glanced at Mikael, lounging on the cushions beside me, seeming none too worried.

Shaking my head, I turned away from him to observe the padlocked cell door for the millionth time, and the guards holding their spears beyond it. If some of them didn't go to sleep soon, I was going to ruin our chances of escape during a bathroom break by peeing my pants.

Just when I thought I could no longer hold it, a guard from the side of our cell approached the two at the front, then spoke with them in hushed tones.

I forced my gaze away from them, not wanting to seem overly curious.

Out of the corner of my eye I saw a guard nod to the one speaking, then the first strode away toward the white tents. A few minutes later, another followed the same process.

I fought the urge to grin. Our lack of escape attempts might have actually made the women comfortable enough to let their guard down, if only a little.

A third guard eventually departed, and I decided it was time to make our move. Three guards was far better than six, and I didn't want to risk any of them returning.

I leaned forward, then used my arms to help push me and my belly to my feet. With a final glance at Mikael, who subtly nodded, I walked toward the barred door.

"I need to use the bathroom," I announced.

One of the guards, a redhead, turned toward me,

then gestured with her spear toward the far corner of the cell. "Use the chamber pot."

I frowned. I'd noticed the small bronze pot, but hadn't guessed what it was there for. "We're a bit . . . modest in my realm." I explained. "Women usually don't relieve themselves in front of men."

"He's your consort," she said, gesturing with a nod toward Mikael. "If a man can get you pregnant, he can watch you urinate."

I shook my head. I couldn't deny that he was my consort now. They might kill him. "Not where I'm from," I argued. "I *require* privacy."

The woman rolled her eyes. "*Fine*, but if either of you try to escape, you will be separated henceforth."

It was a risk I was willing to take if it got me out of this damn cell. I nodded eagerly.

The redhead waved to the single guard stationed at the backside of the cell, facing the jungle, and the woman trotted around the cell toward the front.

"Find Tamara," the redhead instructed. "We require extra guards."

I caught myself before my shoulders could slump in disappointment. The guard trotted away to follow her orders.

So much for only dealing with three guards, unless .. . I glanced back at Mikael. At the moment we only had two, but it wouldn't be long before the others returned.

He glanced briefly at the two remaining women, then nodded. Suddenly he hopped to his feet.

Knowing his plan, I turned back toward the women and blasted them with energy. Mikael dove toward the cell bars, snagging his fingers around the keys at one of the women's belts as they were knocked from their feet by the impact of my energy blast.

He whipped his hand back inside the cell, then through another bar near the padlock. I had a split second to prepare myself, then the door swung outward just as the two women climbed to their feet, spears in hand. Shouting erupted from the nearby tents. We only had seconds to make this escape work.

Before I could even react, Mikael swooped me up in his arms like a child and darted through the open door. His leg swung up, launching his foot into one of the woman's chests before she could ready her spear.

The other woman was faster and lunged for us, trying to force us back into the cell with her weapon. I used every ounce of remaining energy I had left to throw at her, but this time she was prepared for it, and merely staggered upon impact.

Still, it was enough of an opportunity for Mikael to kick her spear away and run past her, just as dozens of female forms hurried toward us, spears raised.

With my body still grasped firmly in Mikael's arms, he quickly pivoted and started sprinting toward the jungle. All I could do was hold on to his neck and cross my fingers that Hecate's barrier was no longer up to trap us.

The women shouted behind us as we entered the

tree line, and I exhaled in relief. No magical barrier stopped us, at least, not *yet*.

Mikael wove between the dark trees and I did my best to keep my feet tucked down, lest I impede our ability to fit through one of the smaller gaps. I was incredibly grateful in that moment that I'd ended up with someone tall and strong like Mikael, and not someone smaller like Faas. I never would have been able to outrun the warrior women on my own.

The shouts began to grow distant as we lost ourselves in the deep foliage, but Mikael did not stop running for a long time. I hoped he knew where he was going, because we still needed to somehow make it back to the World Tree branch to go home.

Eventually, when the night air was utterly silent around us, he slowed, then let me down to my feet.

Unfortunately I was unable to express my gratitude in that moment, because I had to hustle toward the backside of a nearby shrub to relieve myself.

When I was finished, I walked back around the bush to find Mikael scanning the darkness. "I believe we lost them," he observed, "but we should keep moving. Odds are ten to one those women know how to track."

I nodded. "I can't believe we actually made it out, and you didn't even have to use your dagger."

He pouted, then knelt to withdraw the small weapon from his boot. He turned it over in his hand, the blade glinting in the moonlight. "Pity," he muttered, then handed the weapon to me as he stood.

I took the blade, looking at him questioningly.

"In case we get separated," he explained. "I expect you're low on energy now."

I *was* low on energy, but I was surprised he'd give up his only weapon to me.

"We should go," he said before I could question him again.

I nodded, slid the dagger in between my thick socks and the interior of my hiking boot, then we both started walking, though my ankles ached and I felt unbelievably tired.

Mikael glanced over at me as we walked. "Would you like me to carry you further?"

I shook my head, feeling down on myself for needing to be carried so far in the first place. "No, I can walk. Do you know what direction the World Tree branch is in?"

"Yes," he replied, turning his gaze back out to our surroundings, "but we shouldn't go there yet. We need to lead the handmaidens as far from the path as possible, then we can loop back around."

I sighed. If that was the plan, he'd definitely have to carry me again at some point, but I wasn't going to admit defeat just yet.

"I can't believe we actually escaped," I mused again. I'd known our loose plan had been a long shot, but it had gone off without a hitch.

He flashed me a smile. "I never doubted our abilities for a second."

Before I could reply, shouts behind us came into hearing range.

"But perhaps it's too soon to celebrate," he added, then swooped me back up in his arms. He took off at a sprint, his strong legs carrying us tirelessly into the night.

ALARIC PEERED out the dark kitchen window, tired of watching Aila stare in awe at Freyja. Freyja loudly chugged a bottle of water, her flaxen hair trailing down her back. She'd already eaten three chicken sandwiches and was on her second bottle of water.

Alaric glanced over his shoulder anxiously, wishing he could communicate with Faas. Had he found Marcos' trail?

He turned back to find Freyja staring at him, while handing her empty water bottle to Aila.

She stepped toward him. "So," she began suspiciously. "You say Loki simply . . . departed? He gave no reason?" One of her blonde eyebrows lifted, ever so slightly.

He shrugged, acting casual. "He showed up, curious about us, then before we knew it, he was gone."

She tilted her head. "Curious about the Vaettir? That seems a bit silly. We know what you are. *You* are the destroyers of the World Tree."

He frowned. He was wondering when *that* would be

brought up. It had happened well before his time, but the gods had long memories. "Loki's reasons are his own. Do you truly believe he would have shared his motives with us?"

She seemed to relax. "I suppose not," she sighed.

Everyone turned as Alejandro burst through the side door leading into the dining area. He panted, his bronze skin glistening with sweat. He glanced curiously at Freyja for a moment, shook his head, then turned to Alaric. "The shit has seriously hit the fan," he panted. "Tabitha and Maya were on their way to Hillsboro, but they only made it halfway there. All of the cars on the highway are at a standstill, their drivers missing. The girls are running back home as we speak."

Freyja sighed loudly. "*This* is what you get when you mess around with Yggdrasil. It should be *guarded*. Things are slipping through from other realms."

"What *things*?" Alaric questioned. Were Freyja and Loki truly the only gods to come through? Could all of the magic he'd seen in the woods been something *else*?

"Who knows?" she replied with a shrug. "There are countless realms. I cannot be expected to know what dwells in each. Leaving a single branch unprotected is one thing. It takes a certain level of intelligence to reach other branches, but anything with the right type of energy can reach the trunk." She paused as a sudden thought seemed to hit her. "That reminds me. I must ask, *who* regrew the tree?" She flicked her gaze to each of the Vaettir in the room. "None of you possess such power."

Shit, Alaric thought. The questions would inevitably always come back to Madeline. Part of him just wanted to tell Freyja in hopes she'd be more helpful than Loki, but he was hesitant to risk it.

Of course, there was a positive aspect to her questioning. It let him know that Freyja didn't know who regrew the tree, which meant she didn't know someone like Madeline even existed. They had feared the gods would come through the tree to hunt Madeline specifically.

When he didn't immediately answer, Sophie blurted, "We don't know!"

Freyja whipped her narrowed gaze to her. "You're lying," she snapped. "Whoever regrew the tree is responsible for the chaos that will only increase. Perhaps they know of a way to stop it."

"We cannot say who was directly responsible," Alaric began, having an idea, "but we do know Hecate had hand in it."

Freyja's eyes widened. "That's impossible. She was sealed in another realm where she could not reach mortals centuries ago."

Alaric shrugged. "Well she was able to reach at least one, a necromancer claiming to be her direct descendent."

Sophie flicked her gaze to him, silently asking, *What the hell are you doing?*

"Where is this necromancer?" Freyja demanded.

"Our people are trying to track him as we speak,"

Alaric explained, "but I imagine *you* might be far more suited to the job, given you found us so easily."

She nodded. "Tracking is one of my gifts. It is why I was sent to find Loki, though he is equally skilled at eluding me." She placed a hand on her chin, deep in thought. "I'll still need to find the little weasel, but perhaps learning Hecate's plan should be of equal importance."

Alaric nodded encouragingly. "As we don't know Loki's location, finding Hecate's necromancer could at least prove productive in the meantime."

"Yes," Freyja decided. "That is what we shall do. Take me to your trackers."

"Um," Alejandro interrupted, still standing in the dining area, slightly apart from the group, "are we going to do anything about all of the magic rapidly leaking into the world?"

Freyja turned toward him. "If Hecate had a hand in growing the World Tree, I imagine this is all somehow her doing. Learning her plan is the next step to solving all issues."

Alaric couldn't agree with her more. Plus, if Freyja decided to go after Hecate, perhaps Alaric could convince her to take him with. He could spirit away Madeline while the goddesses duked it out.

"Our trackers should be out in the yard," he explained. "The necromancer was here yesterday evening. They hope to pick up his energy signature."

"Energy trackers?" she questioned. "How delightful. Take me to them."

Sophie joined his side as he led the way. She met his gaze more than once, clearly conveying her worry. He was worried too, but he knew in his heart if he wasn't willing to at least take a small risk, he might lose Madeline and their child forever.

WHEN THE SHOUTS could no longer be heard, Mikael finally let me back down to my feet. I guessed it was sometime close to midnight. I felt almost guilty for being absolutely exhausted, since Mikael was the one that had been carrying me for most of our escape. We'd walked through a few small streams on our journey, traveling down or upstream through the water for long distances to conceal our tracks. The handmaidens hopefully wouldn't be able to find us now, unless they could track energy like some of the Vaettir. They didn't seem in any way magical though, just like regular women, so hopefully that meant we were safe.

"I suppose we can rest for a time," Mikael suggested.

My shoulders slumped in relief. I hated to rest when I was desperate to get home, but I really needed it. I'd used up my energy stores fending off the handmaidens, and since we didn't have any food, sleep was the only way for me to recover.

He glanced around the dark woods, then pointed to a

rocky outcropping. "Let us rest in that alcove. That way, we at least won't have the enemy sneaking up behind us."

Too tired to think straight, I nodded, then started walking toward the rocks.

Though close, getting there seemed to take forever. Finally, we sat down side by side, leaning our backs against the hard, cool, stone. I shivered. It wasn't absolutely freezing outside, but cold enough that sitting still was uncomfortable.

I sighed. "What do you think happened to the others? Are they alright?"

He put an arm around me and pulled me toward him, sharing his warmth. "I told you once before that you would know if Alaric were dead. I still believe that to be true."

I sighed again, then closed my eyes. "He might be okay for now, but if Hecate sent them all back to our realm, he could still be in trouble. *All* of our people could be in trouble. Hecate might have it out for the old gods, but I have a feeling she won't care who else gets trampled in her quest for revenge."

"We'll just have to get back there and figure it out," he comforted.

I nodded. "Do you think Loki is still with the others? I'm worried they'll all try to come back here again and we might miss them."

He gave my shoulder a squeeze. "I do not know. I told you we could not trust him. He might not have had his magic in this realm, but he is still an ancient, clever being. Yet, Hecate was still so easily able to separate him from us."

"You're right," I muttered. "We shouldn't have trusted him. You'd think after all the times I've been betrayed, I'd stop trusting strangers."

"You see the good in people," he replied, his voice soft. "That is not a fault."

My eyes still closed, I smiled. "Except when I see the good in mischievous, ancient Vikings. I should probably stop doing *that*."

He snorted. "Now are you referring to Loki, or to *me*?" he asked jokingly, knowing I'd meant the latter.

I chuckled. "Both."

"Ah," he sighed. "Some day I'll win you over."

As I began to drift off, I leaned my head on his shoulder, nestled in the curve of his arm. I distantly felt him place his free hand on my belly as he laid a kiss on the top of my head, but I was too far gone to really consider it.

7

―――――

"Fascinating," Freyja muttered, watching Faas as he stood in the middle of the dark trees bordering their property, his arms held out to either side. "I had no idea the Vaettir had developed such interesting abilities."

"So you truly could not see us at all?" Aila questioned, standing a few paces away from the goddess.

Freyja shook her head, tossing her flaxen hair from side to side. "When Yggdrasil was destroyed, we lost all access to this realm. We could see nothing."

Alaric pondered her answer, watching Faas as he paced around searching for the direction of Marcos' energy. "So," he began, an idea coming to him, "before Yggdrasil was destroyed, did this land have magic like it's experiencing now?"

He turned to Freyja as she shook her head. "The World Tree's trunk originally resided in a neutral space, slightly parallel to this realm, but closer to it than any others. Your kind should not have been able to reach it, nor should any magic have leaked through."

"Then I don't understand," Aila interrupted. "I thought the World Tree was originally destroyed by the Vaettir."

"Indeed it was," Freyja replied, "but they had help from a goddess. They were aided by Hecate."

Faas stopped his search and turned toward them, his face a pale oval in the minimal moonlight. "But then why did Hecate want to regrow the tree, if she was the one to originally destroy it?"

Freyja smiled ruefully. "She did not foresee the power vacuum the tree's destruction would create. She had hoped to sever the old gods' connection from this realm, while she remained behind with her precious women worshippers. Instead, she was sucked through the vacuum and into a nearly dead realm, along with her female followers. She has been trapped there ever since," she frowned, "though apparently her realm is not far off, if she's able to communicate with her descendent."

Suddenly everything made sense. The women in Hecate's realm must have been those who originally helped her destroy Yggdrasil. Now, Hecate wanted to return to this realm and have another try. She would use the tree, then destroy it, trapping Madeline in another realm forever. With Madeline's energy in Hecate's realm, the power vacuum might not exist.

His heart sunk at the notion. He could be wrong, but

it was the only reason he could think of for Hecate to lure Madeline to her realm.

"I have an admission," he sighed. He was still wary of telling Freyja the truth, but he could not risk Madeline being forever trapped in another realm.

Freyja raised a blonde eyebrow at him. "Go on."

"I *do* know who regrew Yggdrasil," he admitted. "I lied because it is someone I love very much, but now that I know the possibility of Hecate destroying the World Tree once more, I feel it is pertinent I tell the truth."

Freyja's eyes widened. "And where is this special someone now?"

Alaric's shoulders slumped. "Loki took us to Hecate's realm. Hecate sent most of us back, but kept Madeline and one other. We have not seen Loki since. He may even be in Hecate's realm with Madeline and Mikael."

"Fools," Freyja hissed, then took a deep breath. "This Madeline, what are her gifts?"

"She was connected to the Morrigan, but not in the way Aila is connected to *you*," he explained. "In fact, we are not even sure of Madeline's origins. She is pure energy in human form."

"The Morrigan?" Freyja gasped. "You're telling me this Madeline has the same energy as Hecate?"

Alaric nodded.

Faas had stopped his search and instead walked forward, listening intently to their conversation, while Aila balked at Alaric behind Freyja's back.

Freyja began to pace across the crunchy fir needles

littering the ground. "All worlds have balance," she explained. "They *need* balance. If what you say about this Madeline is true, she was the anchor that provided energy balance in this realm. She has been born again and again, with her energy never truly leaving. When she traveled through Yggdrasil, she created a vacuum to pull magical energy into this realm. *That* is why the magical flood increased."

"So we bring Madeline back, and the flow stops?" Faas questioned.

Alaric could have hugged Faas in that moment for suggesting such a notion. The magical leak might just be enough motivation for Freyja to help them.

"It's not so simple," Freyja replied, continuing to pace. "I'd wager Hecate *wanted* Madeline in her realm so she could take her place. When Hecate destroyed the World Tree the first time, the vacuum was created because her energy no longer belonged here. There was no room for it, as it existed elsewhere in this realm. Yggdrasil is made of similar energy, which is why it took root in a realm very close to this one. When it was destroyed, the excess energy joined with similar energies in this world and formed the Morrigan. With the Morrigan's birth, there was too much of that type of energy here, forcing Hecate out."

She took a deep breath, pausing her lecture. "*This* time, with that energy, Madeline, already trapped in the realm where Hecate was originally transported, she could destroy Yggdrasil *without* being pulled through.

Yggdrasil will release a measure of that energy once more, but it will likely not be enough to force her out. She could once again sever the old gods from this realm, but this time, she would remain behind, the only godly power to rule over the mortals. The only positive of that situation is that Hecate's presence will likely stop the flow of magic into this world, since she would take Madeline's place."

"Very good," a voice said from behind Freyja and Aila.

Alaric whipped his head to the voice, witnessing Marcos emerge from the trees.

Tallie and Sophie came trotting up behind him, having tracked Marcos' energy back to them.

"Found him," Tallie said weakly, holding a limp finger in the air.

Freyja turned on Marcos. "Hecate's descendent," she observed. "Give me a single reason not to kill you."

He grinned, the expression made eerie on his pale, thin face. "Because *I'm* going to help you defeat Hecate."

Alaric's heart nearly stopped. Had this been Marcos' plan from the start? Had he played them all this whole time?

He balled his hands into fists, wanting nothing more than to kill Marcos himself. Yet, he could not risk it. He could not risk killing an enemy who could perhaps double as Madeline's salvation.

"I think it's time for you to divulge your plan," Alaric growled.

Marcos nodded. "For once, you are correct." He flicked his gaze to Freyja, then back to Alaric.

Tallie and Sophie moved to stand near Faas, both crossing their arms while they awaited Marcos' explanation.

"It was many years ago that Hecate first reached out to me," Marcos began. "She was just a tiny voice in my head that grew loud when I really listened. She began to tell me of her plan to return to this realm. At the time, I was in the employ of Aislin, but Hecate showed me a better path."

"You planned to betray Aislin from the start?" Tallie gasped, the only one among them who had also been one of Aislin's people.

"No," Marcos answered blandly, "but neither was I loyal to her. I have always been kept on the outside, you see. Both as an executioner of the Vaettir, and as a necromancer. I belong more with the dead than the living."

"And we'll gladly put you there in truth if you do not hurry up your explanation," Sophie snapped.

Marcos smirked at her, then continued. "I can skip over much of my explanation, since you seem to have figured out Hecate's plan. For that, I commend you. It took me a while to divine her true motives."

"And yet knowing them," Faas began, "you continued to help her?"

Marcos shrugged. "How do you fight the voice inside your head, a voice that can reach you no matter where you go? She could speak to me so much in my sleep that

I would never sleep again. I had nearly gone mad by the time I decided to devise my own plan."

Freyja narrowed her eyes skeptically. "You were able to devise a separate plan while a goddess resided in your head."

Marcos smiled. "I've always been adept at shielding. Even Madeline could not pry away the layers to my true emotions."

Faas nodded. "She always claimed to feel very little from you. She just assumed you were a psychopath."

Marcos nodded. "Like I said, I'm very talented at shielding. I began to devise a plan of my own to kill Hecate, knowing it was the only way to remove her presence from my life."

"You are a fool," Freyja growled. "You assume you can kill a goddess all on your own?"

Marcos tilted his head, trailing pure white hair across his black-clad shoulder. "No, not alone." He swept his arm to encompass everyone listening to his tale. "That is where all of *you* come into play, and Madeline, of course."

"You know how to get her back?" Alaric questioned, stepping forward.

Marcos nodded. "I led Hecate to believe Mikael was the father of Madeline's child, not you. I needed him to be there to aid in Madeline's escape."

Alaric took another step forward, clenching his fists to keep from lashing out. "You trapped her there on purpose, and without me?"

Marcos smiled, not seeming to sense his impending doom. "It was quite clever on my part, really. Mikael would plan rationally, and would provide Madeline with her best chance of escape. *You* are too emotional. You would have fought off the handmaidens to protect her. You would have been killed, and Madeline would have been left to escape on her own, weakened by her pregnancy."

That gave Alaric pause. Mikael had survived for over a thousand years through rational plotting and scheming, while he'd survived by *fighting*.

"Glad to see you understand," Marcos said with a nod.

"Get to the part where we kill Hecate," Freyja prompted, "lest I kill you and handle it myself."

Still not seeming in the least bit perturbed, Marcos continued, "Hecate will need followers for her ritual, but as she is currently guarding Yggdrasil, she has enlisted me to gather followers in her stead. The Vaettir destroyed the tree with her once, and she would like to enlist them to do so again. The women among us unknown to her will pose as her followers." Marcos gestured to Tallie, then to Aila. "And perhaps a few others," he added, "if there are any you trust. The rest will lie in wait for Madeline's return."

No one argued with his plan. Alaric knew they *all* loved Madeline in their own ways, and would want to help as they could.

"The women and I will delay Hecate's ritual," he

continued, "buying Madeline and Mikael the time they need."

Freyja nodded. "And once Madeline has returned to this realm, Hecate will be weakened. She and Madeline will both share the energy that each would have full force when alone in their own realm. We will be able to kill her and send her energy back from whence it came, and with Madeline back in this realm, the magic vacuum will cease to be."

"Precisely," Marcos agreed.

Alaric met his sister's gaze. She nodded subtly. It seemed the plan was as good as they were going to get. Madeline would be returned to them, and Freyja would keep her alive to keep balance in the realm.

"There's just one problem," Faas observed. "What if Madeline does not make it back on her own?"

Marcos simply smiled. "All great plans must have an element of risk. Without such risk, there can be no great gain. I have faith Madeline will find a way. She has not failed me yet."

Alaric clenched his fists again. He didn't like the idea of risk, but knew there was little choice. If Hecate was guarding the tree, she might kill them before they could travel through with Freyja to retrieve Madeline. If he simply put his trust in Madeline, they could gain the upper hand, weakening Hecate enough to kill her once and for all.

It was the best plan they were going to get, and Alaric

intended to be on the front lines, even if he could not pose as a follower himself.

EARLY MORNING SUNLIGHT crept across my face, waking me. I squinted up at Mikael, his arm still wrapped around me with my head cradled on his chest.

"Good morning, sleeping beauty," he muttered.

I sat up and rubbed my eyes, peering blearily at the surrounding forest. My back ached where it had been leaning against the stone outcropping, and my butt wasn't feeling much better. I sucked my teeth, wishing I had some water. We'd risked a few sips from a stream the prior day, so it wasn't an emergency, but would have been nice. *Coffee* also would have been nice.

Mikael stood, then offered me a hand up. I took it and rose as my stomach let out a loud growl.

I blushed. "We *really* need to either get back home today, or hunt some of those weird little songbirds."

Mikael raised an eyebrow at me. "You've turned into quite an *animal* for a former vegetarian."

"Hanging out with feline warmongers tends to have that effect," I quipped, then stumbled off to go to the bathroom. As I picked my way through the bushes I became quite sure that I never wanted to leave our cozy home again, even when it was overcrowded with other Vaettir.

Mikael was waiting for me upon my return.

"Yggdrasil's branch should be roughly north of us," he pointed. "But we must proceed with caution. It would not do to get recaptured before you can bolt us out of here."

"*If* I can bolt us out of here," I added. "Remember, I've only done it once."

He raised an eyebrow at me as we started walking. "Are you not confident in your abilities?"

I sighed, then shrugged. Was I? I was constantly surprising myself with what I could do, and now that I knew a little bit more about the energy inside me, I felt like more was possible. Still, I'd only been alive for a tiny blip of time compared to many of the other Vaettir, and I'd only been focused on honing my gifts recently. Faas did his best to guide me, but the Morrigan had been the teacher I really needed, and she was dead.

"It will be fine," he assured. "I know nothing will keep you apart from Alaric," he added somewhat bitterly.

Now it was my turn to raise a brow. "Do you have a problem with that?"

He smiled softly. "No. Perhaps I just wish I had such allure."

I stopped walking. "I would travel realms for you too, you know."

He turned to me. "Would you?"

I nodded. "And I know you'd do the same for me."

"And why is that?" he asked.

I narrowed my eyes at him, suspicious of why he was

bringing this up *now*. "Because we're friends," I replied. "I'd do it for Sophie or Faas too."

He sighed. "You're quite dense, sometimes."

I scowled. "I'm just being honest, you don't have to insult me."

He rolled his amber eyes and started walking again.

I caught up to his side, baffled by his sudden anger at me. He *never* got angry with me, but he'd been acting weird for weeks. I grabbed his arm to stop him.

"Why are you acting like this?" I demanded.

He lifted his hands as if to somehow illustrate his point, then dropped them. "It's just frustrating," he explained with forced calm.

"What is?" I pressed, refusing to back down.

He sighed. "The fact that you would travel to different realms for everyone, and I would only do it for *you*."

I blinked up at him, shocked at his admission. Sure, he flirted with me ceaselessly, but that was just his personality. He cared about me like he cared about Aila and the rest of his original clan.

For a moment he seemed at a loss for words, then he grabbed me and pulled me against him, pressing his lips against mine.

My brain completely stopped. Was I seriously trapped in another realm, kissing Mikael while horrible things could be happening to the father of my child? And why wasn't I pulling away?

He released me and stepped back.

I gave him an expression just as dumbfounded as the one before, belying the nervous patter of my heart. "You do realize I'm pregnant with another man's child, right?"

He stared down at me. "Tell me you feel nothing for me. Tell me my feelings are one sided."

I stared up at him, my jaw slightly agape while my lips still burned from our kiss. Could I truly say that I returned none of his feelings? I was already with Alaric when I'd first met Mikael, so I'd put him squarely in the *friend* box.

He smiled. "I knew you couldn't deny it. Come now, let's find the World Tree." He turned and walked away.

"You smug bastard!" I hissed, hurrying to catch up with him.

I was about to go off on a tirade, when he pressed a finger to his lips, his expression suddenly cautious.

I froze.

A moment later, he grabbed me and pulled me behind a nearby tropical shrub. I was prepared to go off on him, then I heard the voices. Two or three women were coming our way, by the sound of it.

Mikael let go of me, but remained in a crouch as he reached into the top of my boot and withdrew the dagger he'd given me the previous night. Knowing his intent, I rapidly shook my head. He raised an eyebrow at me, then sighed.

The women's voices grew closer. They were almost upon us. Suddenly I realized Mikael had been right. He needed to get the jump on them and eliminate them before they could alert everyone else of our location. We would never get to the World Tree branch if we spent all day running away from handmaidens.

"I think I see something over there," one of the women said.

Crap, they'd spotted us, and I'd ruined our chances of a preemptive strike. As much as it pained me to hurt the women, I patted Mikael's arm to get his attention, then nodded for him to go ahead.

They were almost upon us as he rolled from our hiding spot and darted behind a tree.

The first of the women reached the other side of the shrub, spotting me. "There you are," she sighed. "You must come with us back to the sanctum where you'll be safe."

Still in a crouch, I stared up at her.

Without warning, Mikael leapt out behind her, kicking her in the back to knock her to the ground face down right beside me. The other two women charged into view.

As Mikael spun on them, I darted for the fallen woman's spear, snatched it up, then pointed it at her before she could react.

"Don't move," I ordered, pressing the sharp spear-point between her shoulder blade and spine, where the back of her dress draped to show bare skin, forcing her to flatten herself on her stomach.

I glanced up at Mikael as he kicked one of the women's spears from her grasp, then nicked the other in her right arm with his dagger. He rolled out of the way as she jabbed her spear at him. He came up behind her, his arm around her neck, pressing the dagger against her throat.

"Drop your spear," he demanded of the third woman.

She glared at him, then flicked her gaze to me.

"Do it," I ordered, dramatically pressing the spear harder into the flesh of the handmaiden at my feet. A dab of blood emerged.

The armed woman tossed her spear aside, glaring at us both.

"Now get on the ground beside your sister," Mikael instructed.

He glanced at me and I nodded. I'd watch over the two on the ground.

Once my prisoners were in place, my spear on one and my boot on the neck of the other, Mikael used his free hand to undo the leather belt around the woman's waist, his dagger yet at her throat. "Hands behind your back," he ordered.

She slipped her hands behind her back while glaring daggers at me. Mikael tossed his knife aside then grabbed both her hands before she could pull them away. She struggled as he wrapped the belt tightly around her wrists, securing it, then half-dragged, half-carried her toward the other two hostages and forced her to the ground.

My gut twisted at the feel of the women's anger, fear, and humiliation, but we really didn't have any choice. At least Mikael had managed to take them down without killing them. Perhaps I was the only one who'd considered the latter option.

Mikael bound my two captives with their belts.

Standing back a bit, I gazed at the three bound women, face down. "Should we tie them to a tree?" I questioned.

Mikael nodded, then undid his own belt, our only remaining tether. He lifted each of the women as he would a sack of flour, seating them with their backs against a small tree.

"You're fools," one of the women hissed. "When Hecate finds out what you have done to us—"

"She'll be glad you weren't killed," Mikael finished for her. "Truly, you should be thanking us."

The woman turned her glare to me, as if it was all my fault.

Mikael finished securing them, then moved to my side. "Let's hurry. I don't imagine it will take them *too* long to escape."

I nodded. Before I could protest, he scooped me up in his arms once more and began to run.

As the trees whipped by us, I retreated deep into my thoughts. We hadn't had the time to finish discussing our kiss, though part of me was grateful. I loved Alaric, I really did, but I could admit, if only to myself, that maybe I loved Mikael a little bit too.

8

———

Aila sped the truck down the highway toward the beach. Alaric clenched his fingers around his knees hard enough to turn his knuckles white. They'd spent the last few hours of the night planning, and were now prepared to face Hecate.

Glancing in the rearview mirror, he examined Tallie, Maya, and Kira in quiet anticipation. One of the communal cars shared by their clan carried Freyja, Sophie, Faas, Marcos, and Tabitha ahead of them.

Only the women, minus Sophie and Freyja, would be able to approach Hecate. She'd never met Tallie, Maya, Kira, or Tabitha, and they were the only women among the clan that Alaric trusted enough with the truth. They'd all proven themselves the last time Madeline's life had been in danger, even if some had been traitors in the past.

Aila slowed the vehicle as they neared the turn off, then

immediately parked. They'd all need to walk down the path to the tree, since they couldn't let Hecate spot any of the men, or anyone else she might recognize. She would think the women had been found by Marcos to be her new hand-maidens, prepared to once again destroy the World Tree.

When Madeline arrived, *if* she arrived, they'd be ready. There was really no saying how long it would take her to escape. They were simply banking on the idea that Mikael would get her out of there just a day after she'd been taken. After all, Mikael was Mikael, over a thousand years old, and he'd not yet been defeated.

Everyone silently climbed out of the vehicles, shut-ting the doors gently behind them.

Soon enough, they were all gathered together, taking a final moment before they split up.

"Remember what we discussed," Alaric began, eyeing each of the large group in turn. "Delay Hecate at all costs until Madeline can arrive."

Everyone nodded.

"I will assure her there are more handmaidens on the way," Marcos explained. "The ritual would be difficult with so few, so she will be inclined to wait." He glanced at Freyja. "The goddess should not get too close, lest Hecate sense her."

Freyja glared at him, but nodded.

"And don't worry," Sophie added, eyeing Tallie, Kira, and Tabitha, "we'll be nearby." Her comforting words did not seem to encompass Aila, who didn't know what fear was, or Maya, with whom Sophie still had a strained relationship.

A few others muttered comforting words, then they dispersed. Alaric watched as Maya, Tabitha, Kira, Tallie, and Aila followed Marcos down the path that would eventually lead them to Yggdrasil.

Freyja moved to Alaric's side and crossed her arms. "I hope the necromancer is trustworthy, for your sake."

"He's not," Alaric replied, "but Madeline has put her trust in him on many occasions. *She* would tell me to trust him now, and so I shall."

Freyja smirked, but did not comment further. Truly, he was just as worried about trusting the goddess standing at his side as he was anyone else.

I waddled alongside Mikael, deep in thought. After leaving the three handmaidens far behind, we'd slowed our pace to assess our plan. No mention of the kiss was made, which was fine by me. No way was I prepared for *that* conversation.

"Yggdrasil's branch should not be far now," Mikael muttered, slowly creeping forward as he surveyed the tropical trees around us.

"I can feel it," I replied. Stepping lightly, I pushed a strand of my long hair behind my ear. I really didn't want to encounter any more of the handmaidens before we reached the branch. We might not be as lucky as we'd been the first time.

Mikael glanced at me as he continued walking, his stride shorter than it would be without me. "Good. Hopefully you'll have no trouble attuning yourself with its energy."

I nodded, though I wasn't as confident as he seemed to be. I'd only done it once, after all, and I had a feeling once we reached the branch, I wouldn't be able to take my time. We'd have one shot at it before we were captured again.

Mikael held out an arm to stop my forward momentum.

I froze, then in the sudden silence heard what had halted him. Female voices, not far off.

"They must be guarding the branch," he whispered.

I nodded, having expected no less. "So what do we do?" I hissed.

He leaned near me, and my heart skipped a beat at his closeness. I gritted my teeth, angry with myself, and also angry with Mikael for opening such an uncomfortable can of worms.

Seeming to not sense the added tension, Mikael whispered, "I'll lure them away, then I'll try to loop back around and hop a ride with you when you're ready."

I whipped my worried gaze toward him, my earlier thoughts suddenly forgotten. "What if I jump the gun and get sucked in before you return?"

"*Don't*," was his only reply before he took off at a jog.

A moment later, shouts erupted ahead of me, and I could hear the thud of footsteps as the women began to chase Mikael.

"Shit," I muttered, waiting a few seconds before trotting forward as gracefully as I could manage.

The clearing where we'd first landed in Hecate's realm came into view, along with two remaining handmaidens guarding a glittering gold branch reaching down from the sky.

"Double shit," I muttered, skidding to a halt before crouching to observe the two women. I should have guessed not all would run off after Mikael. Both women held spears at the ready. There was no way I was going to be able to fight them. I didn't have enough energy left.

My gaze whipped up as something across the clearing rustled in the bushes. I held my breath as my gaze flicked back to the two women, who'd noticed the rustling. Glancing at each other, they moved to investigate. I wasn't sure what was in the bush, but it was the best opportunity I was going to get. I'd just have to hope Mikael circled back around soon.

As the women approached the still rustling bush, I emerged from hiding and crept up behind them. My heart thudded in my throat with every step. All it would take was one of them glancing over their shoulder and they'd have me.

The bush continued to rustle though, providing me with a better distraction than I'd hoped for.

I continued my slow advance, my eyes trained on the

women. I jumped as a hand darted out from beneath the rustling bush, grabbing one of the women's ankles and pulling it out from under her. She landed on the black soil with a thud as her partner jabbed her spear into the bush. The hand let go of the first women's ankle to grab the spear, then started tugging it away from its owner.

Wildly curious, but running out of time, I hurried across the final small expanse and placed my palms against the dangling golden branch. Just like before, the energy felt familiar to me. It was easy to attune myself. Now I just had to be careful not to jump through too soon.

"Hey!" a new handmaiden shouted, running full speed into the clearing at my back. She barreled toward me as the woman fighting what was in the bush looked to the commotion. Sighting me, she grunted in outrage, then hurried toward me, spearless.

I froze, unsure what to do. I needed to be in contact with the branch the moment Mikael arrived.

Slowing their pace with cautious expressions on their faces, the women closed in around me.

"Do not go," one pleaded. "You will not be safe in your realm."

"Mikael!" I called out, unwilling to remove my hands from the branch. I was pretty sure I could get us out of there quickly at this point, though I might accidentally pull a few of the handmaidens along for the ride.

One of the women reached out to grab my arm, then

turned as Mikael came charging toward us, trailing a whole herd of women in white dresses.

"Now!" he shouted.

I closed my eyes and focused on the most familiar energy I could think of, Alaric.

"Loki!" one of the handmaidens shrieked.

My eyes shot open and darted to the side as Loki pounced out of the rustling bush. He and Mikael reached me at the same time, then the tree swept us up, sending us plummeting toward earth.

I had a moment of silent weightlessness, then my butt thunked onto the sand with Mikael and Loki on either side of me. Several of the handmaidens plunked down around us, then gazed around in horror at the hazy beach.

"What are you doing here!" a woman shouted.

I turned to see Hecate charging toward us, dressed similar to her handmaidens, but with accents of gold at her waist and shoulders. Her auburn hair whipped about in the cool ocean breeze.

My confusion grew as I glanced behind her to see Aila, Tallie, Maya, Tabitha, Kira, and . . . Marcos? What the hell was going on?

Loki and Mikael each took one of my arms as they stood, hauling me to my feet.

"Ah," Loki mused, flexing his hands as he stepped away from me, "it feels good to be at full power again."

"I thought you left us," I accused.

He rolled his eyes. "I waited near that branch for an entire night for you to show up."

"Silence!" Hecate shouted upon reaching us. She paused as she glanced at Loki, shook her head, then took a step toward me. "Go back immediately, Madeline. You are not safe here."

The four handmaidens who'd come through the tree with us huddled behind Hecate, flicking sand from their long dresses.

"The only thing I'm not safe from is you!" I growled, ignoring the nervous looks from Tallie, Tabitha, and Kira, while Maya and Aila stood stoic behind them. "You imprisoned me against my will!"

Hecate sneered, then took another step toward me, but was intercepted by Loki.

"*Old god*," she hissed. "How did you elude me? You should have been powerless in my realm."

Loki shrugged. "Powerless, but not stupid. You should know better than to employ illusions against a trickster god."

Mikael touched my arm, drawing my attention away from the godly standoff to small forms approaching us from further down the beach.

Hecate whipped her gaze toward them. "Freyja?" she muttered in disbelief. She turned around to glare daggers at Marcos. "Have you betrayed me?" she hissed.

He tilted his head to the side. "I never did enjoy having your voice in my mind."

"What would you have us do?" one of he hand-maidens asked of Hecate.

"Take my hands," Hecate muttered, then gestured for the other women in my group to join them.

The handmaidens each clung to her, but the others just stared.

"False followers sent to delay me?" Hecate sighed, glaring at Marcos.

My friends crossed their arms smugly as the forms on the beach neared. I picked Alaric out amongst the group and nearly tipped over in relief that he was alive and well.

I looked back to Hecate. I still wasn't quite sure what had been planned while I was away, but it seemed the Vaettir had set a trap for her. She glared at me with her fierce green eyes.

"It's over now," I said evenly. "Either go back to your realm willingly, or we'll force you there."

"I don't think so," Hecate sneered just as the others reached us.

I felt a wave of power, then Hecate and the hand-maidens disappeared.

I blinked at the now empty space in disbelief, then turned to Loki. "Did you know she could do that?"

He shook his head. "Not in this realm. She shouldn't have such power."

I turned away from him as those speeding down the beach finally neared us. Alaric, Sophie, and Faas, as well as an extra woman I'd never seen before.

"Ah hell," Loki muttered. "She found me."

"Friend of yours?" I asked.

"Fellow Norse deity," he scowled.

I turned away from Loki as Alaric reached us slightly ahead of the others. He swept me up in a hug, nearly crushing me.

"I was only gone one night!" I laughed as he pulled away, leaving his hands at my waist.

"Which could have turned into an eternity," he explained. "Hecate planned on destroying the tree, trapping you in her realm *forever*."

It felt for a moment like my stomach had fallen to my feet. I took a deep, shuddering breath. "I had no idea. I knew she wanted to screw over the old gods, but I didn't realize just how far she'd go."

"Not to interrupt," Faas said as he stepped forward, "but with both Hecate and Madeline in this realm, does that mean that the flow of magic is going to get worse?"

The flaxen-haired woman beside him nodded. "I believe so. It stemmed off temporarily when Hecate entered this realm without Madeline, but now that they both are here, things might become . . . chaotic."

I'd been focused on Faas and the woman, so I didn't notice right away that Loki had been slowly slinking off toward the trees.

"Not so fast!" the woman snapped, whipping her gaze to him.

He froze.

She stalked across the sand toward him. "What were

you thinking, taking Madeline to Hecate's realm? Do you realize the trouble you've caused?"

Alaric put his arm around my waist and gave me a squeeze. "Freyja found us shortly after we were sent back," he whispered in my ear. "She believes you exist to keep balance in this world, and does not wish to destroy you."

I turned wide eyes up to him, then toward the flaxen-haired woman. First Loki, now Freyja? I had to admit, having them both on our side was a sudden, strange relief.

"And you all came here to kill Hecate?" I whispered.

He nodded. "We'd hoped to ambush her as soon as you arrived, since your energy would weaken her, but we'd thought Loki had abandoned us. No one expected him to journey back with you."

I sighed. There was so much going on, but my stomach was twisting in knots for *other* reasons. "Alaric, I —" I began, but Freyja had turned away from Loki to approach us.

"We must formulate a new plan," she explained as Loki slunk up behind her. "*Both* of us," she gestured to him, "will see it through to the end. We need to stem the flow of magic before worse things come through the trunk."

Alaric took my hand, then explained, "It seems having both you and Hecate here throws off the balance in this realm, allowing magics to leak through Yggdrasil's branches to its trunk. The same occurred when you were both in Hecate's realm. Too much or too little of your energy leaves a vacuum. This is the reason you belong here, and Hecate does not. Your energy has been reborn here countless times."

I blearily took it all in as everyone gathered around us.

Aila shook her head, tossing her blonde ponytail from side to side. "What will we do now? Can we leave the tree unguarded?"

Marcos nodded. "Now that Madeline has returned, Hecate cannot risk destroying the tree, lest she be sucked back into her realm. Her only option now is to eliminate Madeline's energy."

Freyja shook her head. "She cannot kill her. The energy will simply be reborn somewhere else on Earth, and in time she would locate it once more."

Marcos smirked. "Not if Hecate tears the energy apart and turns it into something else. Just like she did with Yggdrasil when it was first destroyed."

Alaric squeezed my hand. "We will not let that happen."

"No," Freyja agreed, "we will not."

I gulped. Having a god protecting me was nice and all, but with the threat of not only dying, but having my energy completely torn asunder, I had to admit I was a little scared. The threat of utter obliteration could have that effect on a girl.

9

We had way too many people for two vehicles, but somehow we made it work with six in the car, and seven in the truck. We'd just have to cross our fingers we didn't get pulled over. Luckily, or really, not so luckily, the cops were probably busy with the blackouts and car accidents in and around Hillsboro.

I ended up in the front of my truck, munching on a bag of trail mix, smushed onto the small center seat with Alaric on my right, and Mikael on my left. Fortunately the truck was an automatic, so I didn't have to worry about maneuvering my long legs around the gearshift.

I glanced in the rearview mirror, observing Loki, Freyja, Sophie, and Marcos. Sophie had *not* been thrilled with the arrangement, but the car was crowded too, so she would have been cramped either way. Aila had taken command of the other group, fitting Tallie, Kira, Maya, Tabitha, and Faas all into the car now following us down the highway. Clouds obscured most of the sun, making early midday feel like evening.

Alaric took my free hand and gave it a squeeze, meeting my worried gaze. Our plan was to go back to the house where Hecate would have to go through other Vaettir to get to me, but I hated the idea. Everyone living with us now had risked themselves when we faced Estus and regrew Yggdrasil. They were supposed to be safe after that, but things had only gotten worse.

"It seems the magic leak has sprung anew since Madeline's return," Freyja commented from behind us.

I sat the trail mix bag in my lap and turned to see her pointing out at the trees as we passed them by. I caught brief glimpses of glowing red eyes, staring out at the road.

"What are they?" I breathed, mesmerized.

"Who knows?" she replied. "Something not of this realm, nor of mine."

I shook my head in disbelief, glancing ahead through the windshield. Colorful, animate lights floated across the road, scattering as the truck neared before bouncing toward the trees.

"Will they be sucked back through to their realms once balance is restored?" I questioned.

"It's hard to say," Freyja answered. "I've never experienced anything quite like this in my lifetime."

"And that's saying a lot," Loki added, "because Freyja is *old*."

"Not as old as *you*," she muttered.

"Can't you scoot over more?" Sophie growled at Marcos.

"No," he answered simply.

I sighed heavily, glancing at Mikael, then Alaric, both utterly silent. I *needed* to tell Alaric what had happened, but I needed to get him alone first. Of course, I wouldn't mind postponing that confrontation for a few more days . . . or years, if I even lived that long.

Mikael turned the truck off the highway and onto the street that would lead to our peaceful little road, and even more peaceful home. I *really* hated that I was bringing chaos there. It was supposed to be our safe haven.

We took another turn, then eventually another onto our long, winding driveway.

As we neared the house I noticed other Vaettir standing guard. Alejandro, Sivi, Frode, Rose, and Maya's brother, Dominic, looked primed for war, brimming with weapons and odd looking piecemeal armor.

"Are they on guard because of the magic?" I asked, leaning forward in my seat. "Or did something else happen?"

"We told them to be ready," Alaric explained, "just in case."

We parked and climbed out of the truck as the car with the others pulled up behind us.

Freyja moved to my side, then turned her attention to Loki as he approached. "Go inside with Madeline and

Alaric," she instructed. "Do not leave Madeline's side. I will take a few of the others to inspect the perimeter."

"Ma'am, yes ma'am," he muttered, turning as Alejandro and Frode hurried toward us.

"You're back!" Alejandro exclaimed, wrapping me in his arms, then quickly releasing me.

I nodded. "Yeah, and my return isn't a blessing to anyone."

Alejandro peered down at me, his dark eyes curious, but holding none of the fear that they should.

Alaric placed a hand at the small of my back, guiding me forward. "We'll explain everything once we're inside," he said to Alejandro and Frode. "Tell the others to obey Freyja's commands." He gestured toward the tunic and pants clad woman already approaching those standing guard.

I hung my head as I moved forward, flanked by Alaric and Loki, and followed by Alejandro and Frode. I felt sick to my stomach with guilt. Guilt for bringing trouble to my friends once again, guilt for the kiss, heck, in that moment, I felt guilt for even existing. If it weren't for Alaric and our growing daughter, I probably would have run away from them all.

We made it to the front door. I exhaled a comforted sigh upon hearing the familiar creak as it opened. Stepping inside, we turned toward the kitchen.

"I'll make you something else to eat," Alaric muttered.

I nodded, though I had little appetite. The trail mix

I'd eaten on the ride felt like cardboard in my stomach.

Loki watched me curiously as I went to the fridge and grabbed a cold bottle of water. I still felt dehydrated from our night and morning with scant water in Hecate's realm.

Mikael entered the kitchen near Alejandro and Frode, both of whom took one look at his morose expression and quietly excused themselves, leaving me alone with just Alaric, Mikael, and Loki. My heart pounded, uncomfortable with this particular grouping.

I wasn't quite able to meet Mikael's eyes, and instead distracted myself taking slow sips of my water.

"How do you feel?" Mikael asked, his amber gaze solely on me. "Has Hecate's presence in this realm drained you of energy?"

I put the lid on my half empty bottle and lowered it to my side. With everything going on, I hadn't thought much about it. "I'm not sure," I answered. I turned to Loki. "Should I be able to tell?"

He shrugged. "How should I know?"

I raised an eyebrow at him. "Well have you ever been in the same realm with one of the other incarnations of your energy?"

He stroked his chin in thought. "I'm not sure if such a thing would even be possible. It's why having you and Hecate in one realm is causing so much trouble. There's a certain balance enforced by the universe, but creatures like yourself and Hecate are difficult to constrain."

I wasn't sure how I felt about being called a *creature*,

but I let it go. "Well, I don't think I feel any different, so maybe the universe is on my side for once. Still, we should probably find Hecate before she figures out a way to change that."

"I agree," Alaric said, slipping his arm around my waist. "We should speak to Marcos."

I nodded, then hesitated. I turned toward Mikael. "Would you mind bringing him in? I need to speak with Alaric."

Mikael raised an eyebrow at me. "Are you sure now is a good time?"

I wasn't sure, but I nodded.

Mikael quietly left the room.

I turned my attention to Loki. "Could we have some privacy?"

He shook his head. "Freyja is already pissed at me. I'm not going to leave you unguarded when Hecate might swoop in and steal you again."

I frowned, then turned my attention to Alaric.

He watched me cautiously. "Are you unwell?" he questioned. "Is the baby—"

I held up my hand to stop him. I didn't need the thought of our unborn child to add any more to my guilt. I glanced at Loki again, wishing he'd go away, then back to Alaric.

"While we were in Hecate's realm," I began hesitantly, fighting the sudden urge to vomit, "Mikael and I kissed." I barely managed to squeak out the last words, though I forced myself to meet his gaze. Alaric wasn't an overly jealous man, but he'd had it out for Mikael before this. I had no idea how he was going to react to the news.

He raised an eyebrow at me. "Would you care to elaborate on that?"

I could tell he was trying to shield his emotions from me, but some leaked through. Hurt and anger, flavored with confusion.

I sighed. "It just happened. He was being a jerk, then suddenly kissed me. He wanted me to admit that I have feelings for him."

Alaric inhaled sharply, then slowly let the breath out. "And do you?"

I glanced at Loki again, who watched our conversation curiously, giving us no semblance of privacy whatsoever.

I looked down at my feet. "I don't know. I don't feel about him the way I feel about you, but I'd be lying if I said there was nothing there at all."

I forced my eyes up to see Alaric frowning. "Excuse me," he said, then turned away.

I grabbed his arm, then recoiled at the emotions leaking from him. The hurt and confusion were gone, completely masked by hot rage. I knew his emotions weren't entirely to do with me. Mikael had been the reason Alaric's mother had been executed centuries ago. I was just the straw that finally broke the camel's back.

He gently took hold of my hand and returned it to my side. "I will not kill him," he said evenly, "but he and I must discuss this. Please wait here with Loki."

I shook my head, slightly dumbfounded. "This is my fault," I blurted. "I'm the one in the wrong. Don't blame him for this."

He glared at me. "Please, do not defend him. Not to me." With that, he turned away and stalked toward the side door leading out into the yard.

I turned to Loki, fighting the blush slowly consuming my face.

He held out a hand toward me. "Come sit down, Madeline."

I numbly obeyed, walking toward him.

He rested his hand on my back and guided me back through the entry room, then into the den, flicking on a lamp before we both sat on the sofa.

As soon as I was sitting I buried my head in my hands. "I'm such a fool," I muttered.

Loki's hand alighted upon my shoulder. "You are not a fool. You are simply young."

I turned my gaze up to him. *That* was the last thing I'd expected him to say. "What do you mean?" I questioned.

He shook his head, a rueful smile on his thin lips. "Both of your men are several centuries old. Mikael is perhaps over a thousand, if my senses for such things are correct. They both know themselves quite well, and so, they know exactly what they want."

I frowned. "What does that have to do with anything?"

He sighed. "It means that you cannot hope to know

what you want, when you do not know yourself. You came from unknown origins, and I'd venture to say Alaric is one of your first serious relationships."

"There were others," I argued weakly. There *had* been others, but none that made me feel the way that Alaric did.

He lifted his hand from my shoulder and patted my head like I was a dog. "There's no need to argue. I'm not being accusational, just pointing out a simple truth. And you shouldn't worry. Men that old tend to not react to things the way you would think."

I sighed and slumped back onto the couch. "No, they really don't. I'm afraid I've been in over my head since the start."

He smirked. "Don't worry, you're a transcendent glowing death ball. They're in over their heads too."

I couldn't help but laugh. Loki was the last person I would have expected to give such sage advice, but he had existed a *very* long time. It made sense for him to know a thing or two about relationships.

"Be that as it may," I replied, "I still have no idea what I'm supposed to do now. I have a child on the way, for crying out loud. Having another man in my life should not be an issue right now."

Loki smirked. "Well since you're already in such a pickle, care to add a third?" He waggled his eyebrows at me.

I scowled. "No, thank you."

He chuckled, leaning back against the fluffy couch

cushion. "Your loss."

I rolled my eyes, wishing I had a watch or a phone on me to check how long Alaric had been gone. "We should probably find Marcos and figure out our plan instead of waiting around," I suggested.

Loki nodded, then froze as a scream echoed in from outside. "Or maybe we should see what *that* is about," he decided, then rose, extending his hand to me.

I took his hand, which he grasped firmly, then pulled me up with ease. The scream had been a woman, not a man, but that didn't mean the screamer wasn't reacting to finding her Doyen locked into mortal combat with Alaric. Or worse, with Hecate.

I raced through the house as quickly as possible, but Loki made it outside a few steps ahead of me. We both paused on the side porch, glancing around for the source of the scream. A moment later I heard a scuffle on the far side of the house, and took off at a slow jog with Loki following behind me.

As we rounded the corner of the house, I first noted the source of the scream, Tallie, clearly in a panic as she watched Mikael and Alaric wrestling on the ground. I stood in shock for a moment, taking in the blood on both their faces, and their disheveled, muddy clothing.

"What the hell are you doing!" I shouted.

The men continued to fight, each attempting to get the upper hand. Alaric rose his body a bit from Mikael's, landing a punch to his jaw, slamming his head sideways. Quickly recovering, Mikael tossed him aside with such force Alaric landed flat on his back. Before he could rise, Mikael pounced on him, his elbow drawn back before his fist slammed into Alaric in retribution.

Standing at my side, Loki chuckled. "Perhaps they are not as evolved as I'd thought."

I scowled at him, marched up to the fighting men rolling around on the ground, and blasted them with what little energy I had left, just enough to give them a small jolt.

Alaric rolled off Mikael, then both blinked up at me, stunned.

"I'll ask again," I growled, "what the hell are you doing?"

Alaric sat up slowly, then stood, brushing himself off. "He's manipulating you, Madeline. I could not let it stand."

My scowl deepened. "You said you wouldn't try to kill him."

Alaric snorted. "If I was trying to kill him, he'd be dead."

Mikael finally stood, flicking bits of mud and grass from his dark brown pants. "He wasn't trying to kill me," he assured. "Though I see no need for fighting at all."

Alaric raised a bruised brow and whirled on him. "Really, would you not feel compelled to attack if someone was manipulating the mother of *your* child?"

"Do you really think I'm so stupid?" I hissed, suddenly angry. "I might be *young* in comparison to you, but when a man tries to manipulate me, I know it."

"This is what he does," Alaric growled, gesturing to Mikael. "It's what he *is*."

I shook my head. I knew I was the one technically in the wrong, and I wasn't sure if I had the right to be mad, but I was. He was implying that Mikael couldn't possibly have real feelings for me, and that my own feelings weren't valid. I was just some stupid young girl being toyed with by a manipulative Viking.

"Perhaps we should sort this out later," Loki smoothly interjected, stepping forward.

He distracted me enough to look over my shoulder and see the other Vaettir gathering around to watch the show.

My shoulders slumped. "You're right." I aimed my gaze first at Alaric, then Mikael. "I'm aware that this is all my fault, but no more fighting until Hecate has been dealt with. We were supposed to be finding Marcos to concoct a new plan."

Miraculously, both men seemed abashed.

I turned back to the gathering crowd as Aila stepped forward. "That's what we were coming to tell you. Marcos is unconscious. We do not know what happened to him."

"Of course he is," I muttered facetiously, "because *that's* exactly what we need right now. Take me to him."

Aila gave a curt nod, then turned to lead the way. Sophie, Alejandro, and the few others who'd gathered, watched us cautiously, likely all dying to know why

Alaric and Mikael had been fighting, but I wasn't about to tell them.

Instead, I followed Aila back around the house and toward the front entrance, with Alaric, Mikael, and Loki trailing behind. We crossed the long porch on the side of the house, then skirted around the corner. Freyja was standing in the driveway near Faas, who knelt beside Marcos, sprawled on his back in the gravel.

Freyja turned to us as we approached, her flaxen hair blowing in a chilly breeze that promised rain. "I believe this is Hecate's doing," she explained. "She does not want him to lead us to her once more."

I frowned as I stopped to hover over Faas to peer down at Marcos. "Can *you* track her?" I asked Faas.

He shook his head, then rose. "I might have stood a chance if magic wasn't leaking into the land at an alarming rate. Can't you feel it?"

I raised my eyebrows, then looked over my shoulder at Alaric, Mikael, and Loki. "*Should* I be able to feel it?"

All three shrugged.

"Faas can feel it more keenly since manipulating energy is his gift," Freyja explained, her eyes on me. "The type of magic *you* use has always been here. It's in the earth and trees, and the gentle kiss of death. A bit of added energy would not be a new sensation for you, though I imagine we will *all* feel it soon enough."

"Okay," I sighed. "So whether I feel it right now or not, magic is increasing, and it's making Hecate difficult to track?"

Faas nodded. "I couldn't even track *you* in this chaos."

I turned as Alaric, Mikael, and Loki moved to stand closer to us. "So what do we do?" I asked the group in general. "I'd rather not wait for Hecate to come and squash out my energy."

Freyja nodded. "I agree it is not wise to wait. I think we should journey toward the apex of the magic. I have no doubt Hecate will try to use it."

"The apex?" I questioned. "You mean Yggdrasil?"

She shook her head. "The magic seems to be flowing *toward* something. While I do not know the reason for this, I find it likely that Hecate will try to use it. So, we go to the apex, we find Hecate."

"But what else do we find?" Faas questioned. "There is other realm magic flowing into this land that even the gods are not familiar with. And the only person who could possibly give us a bit of insight is unconscious." He gestured down to Marcos.

Each of us gazed around our small circle, our moods somber. Faas was right, we had no idea what we'd be walking into.

"Well," I began, breaking the silence, "there's only one way to find out. Let's hunt down this apex."

Loki and Freyja both smiled, clearly ready for action. Mikael and Alaric, both battered and bruised, held similar worried expressions. While charging into danger had always been my preferred course of action, it often didn't turn out too well.

10

Once again, we all piled back into the vehicles, though this time we took three. I ate a sandwich in the passenger seat of my truck while Aila drove. I had a second one sitting in my lap. If I didn't have any fresh dead to gain extra energy from, food was the next best option.

In the back seat were Freyja, Alaric, and Loki. The car behind us held Mikael, Sophie, Alejandro, Faas, Frode, and the third vehicle, a forest green SUV, held our other volunteers. That we had so many willing to face Hecate and whatever magics might await us both warmed and chilled my heart. Some would likely perish.

We'd debated on bringing Marcos in his unresponsive state, but in the end had settled on lugging him into the SUV. If he woke up at some point, we wanted him where he could be useful to us.

I finished my first sandwich and reached for the

second one as we drove down the highway, heading toward Hillsboro. There were a few abandoned vehicles on the side of the road, and not much traffic besides.

With one hand on my sandwich, I used the other to fiddle with the radio knobs, hoping for some news updates. After a few ticks of static, a woman's voice came in loud and clear.

" . . . reports of blackouts in Hillsboro reached us right before all communication was lost. Coupled with the slew of recent traffic incidents, the city seems to have come to a virtual standstill. Authorities are currently investigating reports of what we can only believe are illusions: spectral forms, flashing lights, and unknown creatures. A public warning has been issued to not venture into Hillsboro until further investigation can be conducted."

I quickly hit the radio button to shut it off. "Well, that does not sound good."

"Is there a large population in Hillsboro?" Freyja questioned.

"Around 105,000," Alaric replied.

I started eating my second sandwich as I turned to engage the backseat passengers.

"Fairly large, then," Freyja stated thoughtfully. "It could be that the magic is drawn to such a large congregation of people."

"But there are other cities," I countered. "Why here?"

Freyja shrugged. "To quote your earlier statement, *there's only one way to find out*."

I glanced at Alaric in the middle of the backseat, meeting his worried gaze, then turned around, looking out the window ahead of me. We'd hit the outskirts of Hillsboro, and it seemed like a ghost town.

Aila slowed the vehicle, forcing those following to slow in our wake. There were more abandoned vehicles here, some pulled off to the side, but some left obstructing the street. It was only a matter of time until one would block our way entirely.

I nearly jumped when another moving vehicle appeared, a small white car, heading slowly our way. The passengers in the car glanced about warily, the female driver white-knuckling it on the steering wheel. She met my gaze as we stopped our vehicle to let her pass around a truck blocking half of the intersection, but she didn't smile or wave.

I turned my head, watching the white car pick up speed as Aila maneuvered around the truck in the intersection. The passengers of the passing vehicle were likely letting out a collective breath to have reached the outskirts of town. Many others had probably left before them. I hoped they'd be safe, but there was no guarantee. The best way to ensure the safety of others was to snuff out Hecate and stop the flow of magic.

I flinched as a bright flash outside stung my eyes, then narrowed my gaze as a giant column of pulsing light shot up into the sky in the distance.

"What the hell is that?" I hissed.

Aila slowed the truck from a crawl to a stop, and we

all climbed out. Those following us did the same, shattering the near silence with a cacophony of car doors shutting.

I stared at the distant column, then watched as Freyja cast a worried look toward Loki. "It feels familiar, doesn't it?"

He nodded, his expression uncharacteristically somber.

I stepped forward, raising my hand to shield my eyes as I peered at the glowing column, shimmering with a myriad of colors tinting the mostly white light. It was roughly five blocks away, and seemed wide enough to take up an entire two-way intersection. It spanned up into the sky, endless.

Goosebumps erupted across my arms. I could feel what Faas had been talking about now. It was as if I could feel the magic flowing past me toward the column, like the gentle kiss of snowflakes touching my skin. Soft and magical, but full of potentially sharp, harmful energy.

"How are we supposed to face *that*?" Sophie asked, moving to stand near Alaric.

They both turned, then looked at me.

I raised my hands defensively. "Hey, I don't know anything about it. This isn't my type of energy."

"No," Freyja interrupted. "It's mine, or really," she glanced at Loki, "*ours*. The column is formed of magic coming from our realm."

"But how?" I gasped. "And why here? Shouldn't this

be happening around Yggdrasil?"

She glanced at Loki again. "Do you think it could be..." she trailed off.

"Well if it is," he replied, "we're all screwed."

"What is it!" Sophie snapped.

"The Well of Urd," Freyja explained. "We'd thought it had been lost with Yggdrasil, but it seems regrowing the tree dropped it into this realm. Or perhaps it's been here all along, hidden all this time."

"The Well of Urd?" Mikael questioned, keeping his distance from Alaric. "Isn't Yggdrasil supposed to grow out of the well?"

Freyja nodded, gazing off at the light column. "Yes, it once did. Perhaps Hecate's leftover followers hid it after she was sucked into another realm, or perhaps she hid it before destroying the tree."

"So what do we do about it?" I asked. I had never even heard of the Well of Urd, but judging by Freyja and Loki's expressions, its appearance wasn't a good thing.

"The well created the fates," Freyja replied, "the one time protectors of Yggdrasil."

"You mean the Norns?" I questioned.

She flicked her eyes to me, then back to the light. "Yes, that is what they were in this realm."

I stared at the distant light column in awe. "Does that mean the Norns could come back?" I'd put the energy of the last of the Norns into regrowing Yggdrasil. As far as I'd known, that had been the end of their race.

Loki raised an eyebrow at me. "Do you truly believe they still have a place in this realm?"

I sighed, then shook my head. He was right, the Vaettir had abandoned the Norns, and now that the sanctuary of the Salr had all disappeared, they wouldn't even have a safe place to hide.

A scream sliced through the air from the direction of the column, then another.

I started forward instinctively, but Alaric grabbed my arm to stop me. "Let the others go first," he urged.

I looked around to all who had joined us.

Mikael hefted his axe into his hands, a wry grin on his face. "I'll lead the way. Who cares to join me?"

I wasn't surprised when Aila stepped forward first, followed by Frode and Alejandro. A few others stepped forward, including Freyja, while Alaric, Sophie, Loki, and Faas all opted to hang back with me.

I met Mikael's gaze as he prepared to march. I wasn't quite sure what to say. *Don't die*, seemed childish, but *I love you a little bit* was even worse.

My moment was lost as he gave me a wink, then turned with Aila at his side to lead the way.

Alaric took my hand and gave it a squeeze. With a smirk, Loki, on my other side, enveloped his hand in mine.

I glared at Loki, but didn't have time for a scathing remark as more screams began to cut through the air. What had we just sent Mikael and the others in into?

"Let's go," I breathed. "I don't want to be far behind if they need our help."

"Only if you promise not to rush in if they're instantly killed," Loki replied.

"No promises," I muttered, snatching my hand from his to lead our small group forward.

I cast a wary eye around the deserted streets as we crept along cautiously. I could still feel all the excess magic prickling along my skin, and the column ahead was like a heavy weight on my mind.

Occasionally, I caught glimpses of humans hiding in the surrounding buildings, or running through the streets away from the column of light. There were occasional wails of sirens in the distance, but nothing close, not yet.

"I don't like this," Faas muttered from behind me. "This energy feels highly unstable, like it could explode or implode at any moment."

"It's entirely possible," Loki replied. "The Well of Urd is meant to be connected to Yggdrasil. Without it, all of its magical energy has no guidance. It's pure, wild magic."

More screams and shouts became clear as we neared the block where the light column had sprouted.

"Perhaps you should wait here with Loki," Alaric advised, his hand still entwined with mine. "Hecate may be using the well as a trap. Perhaps she wants to use the well's power to destroy you."

"Also possible," Loki commented.

Alaric stopped walking, pulling me to a halt beside him. The shouts and screams near the well grew louder, accompanied by the clang of metal. Mikael and the others were battling something or someone.

Panic blossomed within me, creating a stabbing pain in my gut. I hunched over, cradling my belly.

"What's wrong?" Alaric gasped, placing his hands at my waist to keep me semi-upright.

Searing pain shot through me, emanating from my abdomen. "Something is wrong," I groaned.

Alaric and Loki helped me lower myself to the asphalt. Faas barged in between them, placing a hand on my belly as I curled up on my side.

"Something's going on with the baby," he explained. "I can feel its energy more keenly than I should."

Sophie hovered over his shoulder, peering down at me worriedly.

"You should have stayed in my realm," a voice said from above us. "The influx of magical energy is too much for your child."

I looked up, pain blurring my vision, to find Hecate standing a few feet away, still in her white dress with gold embellishments. Her auburn hair fluttered in the magic surrounding her.

"Time to end this," she purred.

Loki and Alaric moved to stand in front of me, blocking my view of Hecate.

Still grasping my belly, I craned my neck to see

Hecate extend her hand, a shimmering ball of light in her palm.

"The well's wild magic," Loki hissed. "How do you control it?"

Hecate chuckled. "I am the magic of life and death. There is no energy greater than mine." She flexed her hand around the glowing orb.

I cried out as another stab of pain hit my gut, realizing with sudden horror that it wasn't just the wild magic surrounding us hurting me, Hecate was intentionally affecting my baby.

I gritted my teeth, but could not even raise my cheek from the asphalt.

She squeezed the sphere again, and everything went black.

MIKAEL SWUNG HIS AXE, a perfect blow meant to separate one of the handmaiden's heads from her shoulders, but she easily darted out of the way, her entire body shimmering with the white glow of magic as she ducked behind a tree in the small park.

The women he and Madeline had encountered in Hecate's realm were no longer the same creatures. They'd been empowered with magic, and seemed invincible. The bodies of countless humans littered the grass and street around them, not far from the glowing column of light. The humans had been massacred, likely offerings to the death goddess Hecate.

He swung at the handmaiden, and missed once again as she cackled with maniacal glee. There were more than the four women who'd returned with them from Hecate's realm. She must have gone back to retrieve them in the interim.

"Mikael!" Aila shouted, just as something barreled into his back.

He leapt into a forward roll, coming up on his feet to face the handmaiden that had hit him with an impossible amount of force, then lost focus on his foes as Aila screamed.

He whipped his eyes in her direction to see one of the handmaidens, her fist *in* Aila's chest. The fist glowed with magic, illuminating the blood that began to leak forth. As he watched on helplessly, the handmaiden ripped her hand free of the wound, pulling out Aila's heart. Her body crumpled to the ground, dead. A moment of pain consumed him, viewing the lifeless body of the comrade in arms he'd known for so long.

In that moment, all rational thought left him. He screamed in rage and charged the woman still holding Aila's bloody heart in her hand. He vaguely noted that many of his other friends had fallen around him.

He swung his axe into the woman's neck so quickly she had no time to dodge. Before her body could hit the asphalt, he whirled on another handmaiden, this one holding a glowing spear.

She countered his axe with her weapon, expertly flinging it from his grasp. Rather than chasing his weapon, he charged her, landing a kick that sent her spear clanking across the nearby street. He knew this was a losing battle, but he no longer cared. If all of his people would soon be dead, he would die with them, taking as many of their enemies as he could along the way.

That was his last thought as something stabbed through his lower back, lurching him upward. He peered down as a gleaming spear tip erupted through the middle of his chest.

His last thought was for Madeline, a final prayer that she would send Hecate back to hell where she belonged.

11

I woke with a groan, quickly realizing that I was being carried. I squinted up into the sunlight overhead as Freyja's face slowly came into view above me.

"What happened?" I muttered. "Where's Alaric?"

Loki's face appeared beside hers as he walked by her side.

"Go back to sleep," Loki ordered. "We'll keep you safe."

I began to struggle against Freyja's strong arms, though I didn't actually feel capable of standing on my own. "Put me down!" I demanded. "Where is Alaric? Where are the others?"

"Don't tell her," Freyja growled. "We need to transport her to the tree and back to our realm."

Memories came flooding back to me. Hecate holding that glowing sphere, squeezing it to cause me crippling pain. Alaric and Loki had faced her. We'd needed to get past her to help Mikael.

"They're dead," Loki explained, despite Freyja's advice. "We were barely able to get you out of there alive. Now we need to get you to our realm before Hecate finds us. She has connected herself and her handmaidens to the well. They're too powerful."

"You're lying," I accused, renewing my struggles to escape Freyja's iron grip. "We have to go back."

My heart thundered in my chest, making me weak with lack of breath. They couldn't be dead. The Vaettir were strong. Alaric and Mikael and Sophie were strong. There was no way they would fall so easily.

"We have to go back!" I rasped again, struggling against Freyja.

"Put her to sleep," she ordered Loki through gritted teeth as she struggled to hold me aloft.

"You're going to make the death ball angry at me," Loki groaned.

They stopped walking and Loki hovered his hand over me. I screamed. I had to stop whatever he was doing before it was too late.

My scream caught in my throat as a warm sensation washed over me. Suddenly I felt like I was encased in a safe cocoon. The world outside faded. My consciousness slowly floated away.

THE NEXT TIME I awoke I was in a soft bed, piled high with fluffy white pillows. Gentle sunlight streamed in through gauzy curtains lining a large room. I vaguely noted a fire crackling in a nearby fireplace.

I slowly sat up, cradling my belly in my loose, dirty flannel, blearily remembering what Hecate had done to me. Everything ached, but I sensed my child was alright. I lifted my hand to wipe hot tears from my face as I peered around the room, feeling like I was in a dream. Or maybe a nightmare.

My gut clenched at the memory of Loki's words. He had to be wrong. It was some sort of trick. Perhaps he and Freyja had planned this from the start, to make me think everyone was dead so they could smuggle me away to their realm. Although Loki helped Mikael and I once, he seemed the traitor now.

I lowered first one foot to the floor, then the other, flinching as my bare skin touched down on cold tiles. Fighting through waves of dizziness and nausea, I stood.

"You should be resting," said a voice I didn't recognize.

I spun around too quickly and almost fell, but managed to stabilize myself against the bed. A woman with hair that seemed spun of pure gold sat in a small wooden chair in the far corner of the room. She was plump with a rosy complexion and laugh lines at the corners of her blue eyes, making her seem warm and friendly. She wore a simple, pale blue dress, comfortably hugging her ample figure.

"Who are you?" I panted. "Where am I?"

She smiled. "My name is Sif. I have been appointed as your watcher for the time being, while the others figure out what to do about Hecate."

Unable to stand any longer, I lowered myself to the bed. "Am I no longer in my realm? I need to go back before Hecate destroys Yggdrasil." I lifted a hand to my aching head, fighting the urge to pass out. Without me on earth, Hecate would have no reason to delay destroying the tree.

"Hecate does not know where you are," Sif stated soothingly, rising from her seat. "She will not risk destroying Yggdrasil until she has found you."

She approached the bed, her soft leather boots hissing across the tile floor. Reaching my side, she sat down on the mattress by my feet.

"Lay back," she instructed, gently taking hold of my arms.

I shook my head. "I need to speak with Freyja and Loki."

Alaric is not dead, I repeated in my mind, though the sick feeling in my gut told me otherwise. Still, I refused to believe it until I saw for myself. It was the only way I could continue on.

She raised a golden eyebrow at me. "They are both in council. They must not be disturbed."

I started to stand again, but she grabbed my wrist, easily anchoring me down in my weakened state.

"Let me go," I pleaded.

She shook her head. "It is my job to see to your well-being. Interrupting the council would not be wise."

I looked her up and down, wondering whether or not I could overpower her if I really tried. "Wise is rarely the world people use for me," I assured.

Though I was weak, I hit her with a burst of energy.

She lifted a hand and somehow directed it right back at me, never even flinching.

I fell back on the bed, stunned.

"You truly are not wise if you would choose to attack one of the gods," she said as she moved to stand over me. "Now you must rest."

Rest? How the hell could she expect me to *rest*?

"Okay," I lied, scooting up onto the bed. "Sorry."

Seeming satisfied, she nodded, then resumed her seat near my feet on the bed. I wracked my brain for what she'd said her name was. Seef? Kif? I really needed to brush up on my knowledge of the ancient pantheons.

"I'm Madeline, by the way," I offered as I propped a few pillows behind me. Bile fought its way up my throat, threatening to give away my calmness as the act that it was.

"As I said," she replied, "I am Sif."

I took a deep breath, *relaxing*, while inside I was screaming for this woman to get the hell out of my way. If I could find Yggdrasil's branch in this realm, I could go home myself. I didn't need Loki, Freyja, or anyone else.

"When do you think the council will end?" I asked

conversationally. "Will Loki and Freyja be available then?"

She shrugged. "It will likely take all night. You can speak with them in the morning."

I glanced at the sunlight still streaming in through the windows. It wasn't even close to nighttime, let alone the next morning.

"Could I have some water?" I asked, then rubbed my belly. "And maybe some food?"

She gave me a warm smile, then stood and made her way toward the door. Was it truly going to be so simple to get her to leave? My heart beat rapidly as I watched her open the tall white door.

She peeked her head outside and spoke to someone who'd clearly been standing there all along. *Shit*. Not only did I have to deal with Sif, I'd have to face at least one guard.

After shutting the door, Sif returned to her seat in the corner, leaving me alone on the bed. "Try to rest now, for your child's sake" she firmly advised. "A meal and some water will be here soon."

I repositioned myself more snugly against the pillows, trying my best to appear at ease.

A few minutes later, there was a knock at the door. Sif answered it, then retrieved a tray being handed in to her. The door shut again, and she approached the bed.

"Just porridge and water for now," she explained. "Something easy to digest in your weakened state."

I nodded, then gratefully took the bowl and glass

from the offered tray. The steaming bowl of porridge *did* look good, but I had better things to do than eat it.

I sat the glass of water on the bedside table, then held the warm bowl up to my face, as if to take a sniff of the mealy aroma.

Sif smiled and lowered the tray to her side, clearly pleased I was finally cooperating.

Without warning, I flung the bowl at Sif, splattering her with piping hot sludge.

Sif screeched, but I didn't have time to pay attention to her reaction. I rolled off the bed, grabbing the glass of water as I found my feet, then used the momentary distraction to slip past her.

I hurried toward the door, willing myself to not stumble, even though I felt a bit like I was going to hurl. Reaching the door, I flung it open with my free hand, then splashed the full glass of water into the face of the man standing guard.

While he sputtered, I chucked the empty glass at him, then turned and ran the other way with Sif yelling behind me.

Pain shot up through my heels as my bare feet pounded across the tile floor. Every step made me feel like I was going to faint, but I kept going, barely observing the gleaming tiles and flawless white walls of the hallway I'd entered.

I skittered around a corner with Sif and the guard calling after me. I'd never elude them long enough to find Yggdrasil's branch, so I'd just have to find Loki and Freyja instead.

I rounded another bend as the guard caught up to me, just ahead of Sif. I whirled on the man before he could grab the back of my shirt, then slowly edged away, my hands held in front of me to ward him off.

Sif glared at me, her face and dress streaked with the remains of the porridge.

"You do *not* want to fight me," she growled.

Voices caught my ear, muffled by a nearby door. If I could just make it in there, maybe I'd find someone to help me.

I must have flicked my gaze to the door, because Sif snapped, "Don't even think about it!"

Knowing this would be my only chance, I threw caution to the wind and lunged toward the door, grabbing the heavy iron handle and throwing it open. The guard grabbed the back of my shirt, but I was already stumbling inside.

Both of us froze at the sight of thirty or so people, all dressed in fine tunics and pants, and some in dresses. They all stopped speaking to stare at us. Sif hurried into the room, grumbling under her breath.

As the guard loosened his hold on my shirt, I scanned the room until I saw Loki and Freyja, then marched toward them.

"I need to go back to my world *now*," I demanded.

Freyja and Loki both looked at each other, then back to me.

"Madeline," Loki whispered, leaning forward, "we are in the middle of a vote to determine what to do with your realm, and what to do with *you*."

I glanced at everyone staring at us, then back to Loki and Freyja. "Well it's *my* realm and *my* . . . me, so maybe I should have a say in things."

"Madeline," Freyja groaned, "you're going to get yourself killed."

"If you're not going to let me go back and find Alaric and Mikael," I hissed, "I'll gladly die."

I put my hand on my belly the moment I said it, forgetting I was speaking for two, but it was too late.

"Let the mortal speak," a man said from behind me.

I turned to look up at him. He was standing behind a podium near the center of the gathering, raised higher than everyone else.

"Present yourself, child," he instructed, gesturing to the open space of red carpeting below his podium.

"That's Odin, you fool!" Freyja hissed at me, but it was too late, I'd apparently caught the All-Father's attention.

With a wary glance at Loki and Freyja, I approached Odin. He had long, silver hair, nearly down to the waist of his silver brocade tunic, yet he didn't seem old. He seemed fit and robust, with only a few wrinkles to give him a fatherly air. The only blemish to his appearance was a missing eye, uncovered by a patch as one would usually expect.

Not quite sure what to do, I approached, doing my

best to avoid staring at his empty eye socket. I reluctantly gave something that could be considered a curtsy, then met his one blue eye.

"Hello," I began hesitantly.

Everyone in the room continued to stare at me, some with jaws slightly agape. Sif had moved to one edge of the gathering, partially hiding herself behind some of the others. The guard who'd chased me had quietly escaped the room while I wasn't looking.

I peered up at Odin and bit my lip. "I did not come here voluntarily," I explained. "All I want is to go back to my world and save my loved ones."

"Your loved ones are dead," he said matter of factly, "and your world is nearly lost. Hecate has placed an entire city within a bubble of power that will only continue to grow. The magic will spread, slowly reclaiming the land. Our next action will be to sever our connection to the World Tree, lest Hecate use the Well of Urd to destroy us all."

I felt like I'd been stabbed in the gut. They couldn't really be dead. They *couldn't* . . . yet, something inside me told me they were. Mikael had always assured me I'd know if Alaric was dead, and I did know it. I knew it with Mikael too.

I could barely keep myself standing as acceptance finally hit me, but I forced a steady breath. There had to be something I could do. At that moment, I didn't care about my realm. I only cared about what I'd lost.

Odin watched me absorb his words, then added. "Unless you have a better plan?"

My thoughts raced. There had to be *something*. If only I could go back in time to keep their deaths from occurring . . .

I turned my gaze up to Odin, my eyes wide. "I do have an idea. I want to use Yggdrasil to go back in time and prevent Hecate from obtaining the well."

Gasps erupted around the room.

Odin narrowed his pale eye at me. "Changing the past is forbidden," he scoffed. "What's done is done."

I fought back tears. I was going to change the damned past whether he wanted me to or not, but it would be a lot easier with the cooperation of the gods.

I nearly jumped as Loki moved to stand behind me. "And is severing one of the World Tree's branches not forbidden?" he asked slyly.

Odin's glare deepened. "It is a necessity, unless you'd have us all destroyed."

Loki tilted his head. "So you would rather commit sacrilege yourself, then allow a mortal to travel back in time?"

Odin rolled his eye. "You truly think a single mortal, traveling back by herself, could thwart Hecate?"

I watched as Loki grinned. "Yes, I do."

Whispers erupted around the room, but surprisingly, Odin smiled. "In that case, I'll offer you *both* a deal. I will allow the mortal a single day with access to Yggdrasil. She may go back in time . . . if she can actually manage it," he laughed. "If she fails in her task," he leaned forward to look down at Loki, "then *you* will be the one to sever Yggdrasil's branch, and you must also kill the mortal."

Loki simply smiled, even though we were talking about my death. "Deal."

I gulped. I had hoped maybe Loki and Freyja could come back with me. Alone . . . well I wasn't sure what good I'd do alone, but damned if I wouldn't try.

12

———

"You're both fools," Freyja hissed as the three of us walked down the hall.

Loki smirked. "I've been called far worse."

"I have to admit," I cut in, "When I came up with my plan, I'd hoped you both would be coming back with me."

"It is forbidden for the gods to travel back in time," Freyja huffed. "We exist somewhere in all times. It could prove disastrous to leave one plane of time absent of our energy, while doubling that influence at a point in the past. It could change *everything*."

We reached the end of the hall, and entered a large room.

I had to stop and stare. The tall stone walls were lined from top to bottom with weaponry. Massive swords, axes, daggers, and things I didn't even have names for gleamed in the artificial light. The far wall was rimmed with bows, some taller than I was, stacked beside bushels of sharp-tipped arrows.

"The least we can do it outfit you properly," Freyja muttered.

"You won't have much time," Loki began, moving past us to select my weaponry. "You'll need to focus on returning to the time where you, Mikael, and I were trapped in Hecate's realm. If you can access the well before her, you might just stand a chance of using its powers against her."

I listened intently to his every word. I'd only traveled through time using Yggdrasil's power on my own once, and that was to bring Alaric, Mikael, and myself forward from Viking times. I had no idea if I'd actually be able to reach the correct time on my own.

Loki returned from the wall and handed me two knives the length of my forearms and a lightweight sword.

"I'm not good with swords," I explained, taking the items in hand. In truth, Alaric had given me a few lessons, but I'd never quite gotten the hang of it.

"You'll feel safer having a sword," he explained. "Just keep the pointy end away from yourself."

I nodded, then affixed the sheathed daggers to my belt with the attaching leather ties. Freyja found a harness for the sword, then helped me affix it around my torso, the straps crisscrossing over my round belly. I was sure I looked ridiculous, but Loki was right, I did feel a bit more confident with the weight of the sword on me.

Without permission, Freyja began winding my hair into a tight braid to fall down my back, securing it with a thin leather cord.

Dropping my hair, she walked around to face me, placing her hands on my shoulders, eyeing me intently. "Now remember Madeline, change nothing that needn't be changed. Some deaths may be unavoidable. What is most important is that you access the well's magic *before* Hecate, then use it to destroy or disable her."

I nodded too quickly, feeling dizzy. Since I'd first met the Vaettir, I'd always gone into these life or death scenarios with backup. I'd never had to depend entirely on myself. I was less than confident about it.

Loki herded Freyja out of the way so he could take her spot. "After you kill Hecate, make sure you return to this exact time," he explained. If you don't . . . well, I actually don't know what will happen, but I imagine if the you that exists right now never comes back to the present, you may not exist moving forward at all."

I gulped.

"Plus," he added, "I stuck my neck out for you. Do not let me incur the punishment that will result should you fail to return. I'd rather not be known as the slayer of Yggdrasil's branch for the next few thousand years. I already have enough nicknames to keep up with."

"I promise I'll return," I said, secretly praying that I wouldn't end up a liar.

"Good," Freyja and Loki both said in unison.

They both looked at each other, then nodded.

"To Yggdrasil's branch!" Loki announced, lifting a finger into the air.

I wished I could be as enthusiastic as he, but at the moment I felt like my entire stomach was going to crawl out of my throat.

Fingers crossed that was the worst thing that would happen to me in the next twenty-four hours.

ONCE I WAS FED and fully outfitted with my weapons, and a borrowed brown leather coat that was unbelievably soft and seemed handmade, Freyja, Loki, and I made the short journey to the World Tree branch, followed by a few of the more curious gods.

The branch wasn't far from the massive estate where I'd woken up. The shimmering gold appendage dangled down over an ornate, well-kept garden, its flowers in full bloom despite it being winter in my realm.

A heavy golden fence surrounded the entire area, with guards at every corner, and four by the gate.

Odin waited with them, gesturing for the guards to let us in without a word.

Once we were through the gate, I approached the branch, craning my neck to stare up at it. It didn't dangle as low as the one in Hecate's realm. We were lucky I was tall, lest one of the gods need to lower himself by hoisting me up on his shoulders. I tugged at the loose white blouse and tan suede pants I'd been given uncomfortably, nervous about what was to come.

Freyja turned her gaze away from the branch to wrap me in a quick hug. When she pulled away, her sky blue eyes held unshed tears.

"I've always liked the mortals of your realm," she muttered. "Do be sure you save them."

"And don't forget to save yourself," Loki added, patting the top of my head.

I sighed heavily, then stepped forward. If I only had twenty-four hours, I needed to leave as soon as possible.

While Odin and the other gods watched on, I lifted my arms above my head to grasp the end of the golden branch. A few onlookers snickered, and commented that there was no way I'd actually be able to use Yggdrasil on my own.

I tuned them out.

Closing my eyes, I focused on the branch, tuning into its energy. Despite the changes Hecate was making in my realm, it still felt the same. A hint of Mara, the Morrigan's energy flowed through me, like a hug from an old friend.

I concentrated on the time to which I wanted to return, focusing closely on the events that had transpired before Hecate left her realm.

Suddenly the sunlight left my face, then everything went dark. The feeling of weightlessness consumed me. I crashed down into the damp sand next to someone's feet.

I scrambled upward, fearing imminent attack.

"Madeline?" the man above me questioned. The familiar voice drew my attention upward.

"Silver?" I questioned in disbelief, looking him up and down.

He wore his usual thin white slacks and cream-colored coat that would have seemed over the top on anyone else, but on him, just seemed right. His gelled black hair didn't have a strand out of place, despite the cool ocean wind.

"Madeline?" he questioned again. "Why have you come back without Mikael?"

"There's no time," I blurted, grabbing him by the arms. "Did Mikael and," I hesitated, "the others travel through the tree? Have any come back yet?"

"Yes," he replied hesitantly. "I've been watching you from afar ever since Loki appeared, so I'd know when it was safe to return. I could hardly believe my eyes when I saw you take everyone up through Yggdrasil. Then Alaric, Sophie, and a few others returned. Once they left I approached to observe the tree, wondering where you and Mikael had gone."

I lowered my hands, wondering how I was going to get him to believe me.

I bit my lip, then took a deep breath. "I'm not able to explain everything right now, but I need you to trust that if I don't get to Hillsboro soon, *everyone* is going to die."

He stared at me. "You're going to have to give me a little bit more than that."

"I can't," I replied. "Just know that the gods are

involved, and you're better off not knowing. Silver, I need you to help me."

He glanced up at the tree, then back to me, seeming to think it over. Finally, his decision came. "Just tell me what you need."

I exhaled in relief. "Drive me to Hillsboro. I'll try to explain a little more on the way."

He nodded. "I have a vehicle hidden on the other side of the highway. It's a bit of a walk."

"Let's hurry," I replied, but he was already walking in his usual long stride.

I hustled to catch up with him. I'd always found Silver's cowardice a little annoying. You couldn't trust a guy that would run off at the first signs of danger. Now his faults that landed me before him might just save us all. I'd have to make a promise to myself to never make fun of him again...at least for a little while.

SILVER SPED down the highway in his little red sports car while I shifted in my seat again, trying to find a comfortable position with two daggers at my hips and a small sword down my back. We'd make it to Hillsboro in another eight or nine minutes, though I knew we probably wouldn't be able to drive the whole way since this was the same day that Tabitha and Maya had gotten stuck in traffic caused by the blackouts and other strange occurrences. Once they'd hit the standstill with cars behind them, they'd had to walk back toward home until someone was able to pick them up.

Just as I thought it, the edge of the standstill traffic came into view.

"Shit," I muttered.

Silver glanced at me as he slowed the car. "Perhaps we should call Alaric," he suggested.

My heart stuttered at the name, but I shook my head. He was alive in this time, and I was going to keep him that way.

"I have to do this alone," I explained. "Just get me as close to the city as you can and I'll take it from there."

It would have been so much easier to tell him that I needed to change the past as little as possible, and that I wasn't going to risk everyone dying again when Hecate showed up, but having him give me a ride was changing the past enough already.

Silver maneuvered through the first abandoned vehicles as we approached them, but eventually had to stop. There was no way his little car was going to make it off road.

I sighed. "Okay, I'll try to walk from here. You should go back to doing exactly what you would have been doing had I not shown up."

He blinked at me. "I cannot leave you alone *now*. Not without any of the others to protect you."

I raised an eyebrow at him. "Forgive my surprise, but you aren't exactly the *run headfirst into danger* type."

He glared at me. "Be that as it may, I know Mikael

would hunt me to the ends of the earth if anything happened to you, when I could have prevented it."

"I really don't think he'd kill one of his oldest friends," I countered.

Silver shook his head and opened his door. "If you don't believe he'd kill me for you, you are incredibly naive."

I opened my mouth to argue further, but he stepped out of the car. Shaking my head, I did the same. We were running out of time, and I couldn't waste any more trying to make Silver stay behind.

I straightened my leather coat, feeling oddly stiff with the small sword strapped to my back, its hilt peeking up from within the coat's collar.

I scanned the empty cars and streets beyond, once again confused about how *still* things were. Where had all the people gone? I knew many would be in hiding with all of the magic seeping into the world, but shouldn't there at least be looters out taking advantage of catastrophe?

Silver walked around the car to stand by my side, his expression grim. "Where do we go from here?"

I shook my head, trying to remember where the light from the Well of Urd had erupted. "There," I said after a moment, pointing roughly northeast. "I need to go somewhere over there."

I started walking despite the trembling in my knees. What if Hecate had the well in her possession previously, and had brought it here with her? I might just being going to investigate an empty street.

Silver walked beside me for a few minutes, then sighed, exasperated. Before I could protest, he picked me up like a child. "Forgive me, but you are *very* slow, and I'd rather like to get this over with. There is a strange aura in this place, an aura of death that sticks to my skin like tar."

I scowled up at him, but time *was* of the essence, so instead I said, "Take me over there." I pointed a few blocks down to where I was pretty sure the well had been. I vaguely recalled Mikael and the others running in that direction to investigate.

He looked to where I pointed, then down to me. "Much death has occurred in that direction."

"Recently?" I questioned. Was I too late? Had I been sent back to the present, and not the past? Was everyone I knew already . . . dead?

"Very recently," he explained. "*Human* death."

I guiltily exhaled in relief. Human excluded Alaric and Mikael. "Take me to it."

With a sigh, he started running with me in his arms. It only took a few minutes to reach a small, vacant park. Silver let me down to my feet and we both glanced around.

The trees rustled in the slight breeze, sun filtering through their branches to illuminate the freshly cut grass. It was then that I noticed the bodies.

Roughly thirty feet from where we stood laid the first

corpse, a young woman. Beyond her, many more had been slaughtered. The scene was made even more grotesque by the pristine half of the park near where we stood.

I walked toward the bodies with Silver following behind me like a silent shadow. As we moved along, I noticed more bodies further down the street.

"What happened to them all?" I muttered.

"Death magic," Silver replied blandly. "Their deaths were used in some sort of ritual."

I scanned the bodies we passed, fighting the urge to vomit. Their deaths had happened so recently, the bodies were likely still warm.

I hated the little tickle of power I began to feel as I walked amongst them. Their souls would not be trapped like Vaettir, but death was death, it had an energy all its own.

I ignored the wisps of power reaching out to me, and the echoes of pain I could feel from the bodies. They'd all suffered before they'd died.

"What kind of ritual leaves behind so much energy?" I questioned distantly, not turning to look at Silver as I asked it. It was too difficult to tear my attention away from our surroundings.

His voice sounded several feet to my right. "We must venture downward to find out."

I stopped walking and turned toward him. He was standing near an open manhole in the street bordering the park.

I shook my head. "Oh, no way."

He nodded, then peered down into the hole. "Whatever ritual was begun up here, it was taken down into the earth."

I swallowed the lump in my throat. I *hated* small, dark places, especially ones filled with water and possibly sewage.

My leather coat flapped gently against my back as I forced my feet forward, avoiding the corpses between us, to reach Silver's side. I peered down into the darkness.

"Do you smell any sewage?" I questioned.

"No," he replied, shaking his head. "I believe this to be a rainwater canal, though it is now a biohazard with all of the bodies."

"More bodies?" I questioned breathily.

He nodded, then gestured down to the tunnel below. "Ladies first?"

I took several shallow breaths, fighting the urge to panic. I might have been a big, glowing death ball, but fresh corpses in water in the dark was not my idea of a good time.

I knelt down to touch the metal ladder mounted on the interior wall of the tunnel, then turned and put my right foot on the second rung. With a deep breath, I lowered my left foot in below it.

Not for the first time, I felt like I was metaphorically diving into the abyss, but the feeling of doing it literally was a new sensation of fear entirely.

13

Nothing attacked me as I continued my decent through the manhole into the rainwater canal. Silver climbed down the ladder right above me. My soft-soled brown boots touched down on concrete.

I released the ladder and quickly stepped aside to make room for Silver. In the small amount of light provided by the open manhole, I could see the beginning of a narrow concrete passageway. On one side a walkway connected to the platform supporting the ladder, and on the other was a low canal, running with just a few inches of water. I shivered, glad for my leather coat, and did my best to ignore the dark shapes in the water, more corpses.

Silver reached the bottom, then squinted in the limited light. "There's something down that way," he whispered, pointing.

I strained to see in the darkness, then shook my head. "I can't see that far."

"Follow the walkway," he instructed.

I scowled at him. "You know, for someone afraid of Mikael's wrath, you are not being terribly protective of me."

"If there is something in here that could kill one of us instantly, I'd rather it be you," he explained. "At least in that case, I'd still stand a chance of surviving and eluding Mikael. However, if I am able to protect you without sacrificing myself, I will."

I sighed, then started walking, stepping carefully as the light behind us receded. I kept one hand against the smooth concrete wall to ensure I didn't veer too far and fall into the shallow canal. I wouldn't drown, but I'd likely break an ankle, or maybe even my neck.

As we crept along, a thrumming energy became apparent. It was weak, but constant, almost how I'd imagine it would feel to be near a massive generator.

"Just up ahead," Silver whispered. "The center of the canal has been destroyed."

I slowed my pace, straining to see, but we were in almost pitch blackness now. If something decided to attack, we'd be goners.

I gasped as bright light cut across my vision, blinding me. I blinked rapidly, shielding my face with one hand as my vision slowly returned, then glanced toward Silver to see him holding a small penlight.

"You had that this entire time?" I growled.

He nodded, not seeming to comprehend my ire. Instead, he shone the light toward the center of the canal, then pointed with his free hand.

I turned to where he'd directed his light, then shook my head, confused. The concrete of the canal had been obliterated, forming a hole that took out part of the walkway ahead. The water must have been so shallow because it was all draining into the hole.

"Well what the hell are we supposed to do now?" I muttered.

He raised an eyebrow at me, his face barely visible in the meager illumination provided by his penlight. "Ladies first?"

I glared at him. "If I survive this, I am *so* ratting you out to Mikael."

He snorted. "If you survive this, it will likely only be because I accompanied you."

I huffed in irritation, then held out my hand. "At least give me your light."

He hesitated, then relinquished the penlight to me.

Not wanting to waste any more time, I approached the ruined edge of the walkway, sweeping the light across in hopes of finding an easy way down into the hole.

The way down was littered with debris sunken into mud slick with moisture, but it looked doable.

Saying a final prayer, I sat down on the crumbling edge of the walkway, smoothing my coat under my butt, then lowered myself into the muck below. Once I had steady footing, I shined the light further into the hole.

It opened up into the earth at an angle, almost like the entrance to a cave. After further observation, I realized it *was* a cave. The hole had been blown into the concrete and the earth below to reveal a massive natural cavern.

Silver hopped down beside me with the grace of a cat, not a strand of black hair out of place, then took a few steps forward, having no difficulty navigating the debris.

I sighed, then started shuffling down the incline. I reached the edge of the hole into the cavern easily enough, but there was a pretty big drop down to the wet cavern floor.

"Okay, you're actually going to have to help me with this part," I said, shining the light downward.

"Are we sure we want to go down there at all?" he questioned.

I nodded, but didn't explain. I was pretty sure I was changing the past more than necessary in taking him with me, but there was no way I'd get down into the cavern uninjured without his help, and I was nearly positive by this point that the well was below us. It had to be done.

Without another word, Silver hopped down into the cavern, bending his knees to absorb the impact of the fall. If the floor was slippery, he didn't show it. He straightened, then looked up at me.

"Can you lower yourself down slowly from the ledge?" he questioned. "I fear you might squish me if you jump."

I rolled my eyes. "Just don't let me fall," I grumbled, putting the penlight in my mouth so I could lower myself to my hands and knees.

Feeling ridiculous, I turned around and lowered one foot down off the edge, bracing myself with my hands and other knee.

"-an yew weach me?" I muttered around the penlight.

I received my response in the form of a hand around my foot. Silver braced my weight as I awkwardly wiggled onto my side and dangled my other foot down. My hands slipped and scraped across the mud and debris as he held both my feet and continued to lower them.

Soon enough I was hanging from my fingertips, praying I didn't lose my grip at the wrong moment. Silver's arms wrapped around my hips, then slid up toward my belly. I closed my eyes and let go just as his knees bent, landing my feet on the floor. He released me, then stumbled back a few steps.

"You are very heavy for a woman," he muttered, regaining his composure.

I took the penlight out of my mouth, then turned to face him. "That's very sexist, and I'm also *pregnant*, in case you hadn't noticed."

I walked past him, shining the light around the dark cavern for what I sought. My boots slid on the slick surface and I nearly lost my balance, but Silver caught me before I could fall.

"I told you I would save you," he quipped before releasing his hold on me.

Before I could respond with a scathing remark, he asked, "Do you feel that?"

Now that he said it, I *did* feel something. The pulsing energy I'd felt above had increased. We were definitely in the right place.

I continued forward, reaching a bend in the cavern, then lowered the light. There was a faint glow emanating from the path ahead.

Without thinking, I hurried forward. This had to be the well. If I could find a way to use it before Hecate arrived, I could defeat her.

There was an *oof* sound behind me, and I skidded to a halt and whipped around. Silver lay on the cavern floor, unmoving.

"How are you here?" a woman's voice demanded from behind me.

I whirled around again, nearly dropping my light to take in Hecate, standing by herself. A few feet behind her was a massive bronze cauldron, spilling forth dull light from its basin.

I opened my mouth, but wasn't sure what to say. As far as Hecate was concerned, I was recently trapped in her realm. In fact, the me from this timeline should still be there until tomorrow morning.

Her green eyes narrowed in the dull light provided

by the well. "I will return you to the tree, and you will go back to my realm where you'll be safe."

I frowned. "You don't honestly expect me to believe at this point that you care about my safety."

Her brow furrowed. "You did not choose to be born with my energy inside of you. As far as I am concerned, you are like a long lost sister to me. I do not wish you harm."

"And what about all those people up there?" I gestured to the ceiling of the cavern. "Did you wish *them* harm?"

She smirked. "Sacrifices had to be made to create the power needed to unearth the well. I left it in a sacred place long ago, and the mortals boldly chose to build a city atop it."

I resisted the urge to glance behind me at Silver. I hadn't heard him move, and sincerely hoped he was still breathing. Regardless, I couldn't help him just now. I needed to find a way to get between Hecate and that well.

"I'm sure the *mortals* had no idea the Well of Urd was down here," I explained, then bit my tongue.

Rage glittered in her eyes. "And just how do you know that this is the Well of Urd?" She gestured to the massive cauldron behind her. "Unless Loki told you?" she added. "Did *he* bring you here?"

"I came on my own," I answered honestly, "to bring you back to your realm. You've upset the balance here."

She scoffed. "*I've* upset the balance? *I* don't belong

here? Do you know what the old gods did to me? I was a peaceful nature spirit once. *Here*. The gods and men alike believed I did not belong on this earth, but I *am* this earth. I am death and creation." She clenched her fist as if grasping for something, then released it. "The gods feared what they could not control," she continued, her voice softer. "They wanted to force me to live in their realm, for gods could not toy with the lives of mortals. But I am *meant* to be here." She pointed to me. "*You* are the imposter."

I shook my head. "I was born here. I've always lived here." I left off that Freyja believed I belonged on this earth. Hecate didn't yet know that Freyja was involved.

Hecate shook her head. "I destroyed Yggdrasil so they could not send me away, but that created new energy to replace me, for trees like Yggdrasil are of *this* earth. When that new energy arose, I was cast out. I was forced into a nearly dead realm with my followers, and the Morrigan took my place on earth. She tormented mortals. She was selfish just like a human. I watched over the land from a distance until she destroyed herself, retreating in spirit to another realm. I'd hoped I could find a way to return, but another was born in her place, and then another after that, eventually leading to *you*." She scowled. "I knew it was only a matter of time until my energy was reborn into one of the Vaettir. A being who could potentially live forever, stealing my place on this earth. So you see, *I* am the one who belongs here, and *you* should not exist."

Her words cut through me like a knife. I wanted to argue, but somewhere deep down, I knew she was right. I knew I had never truly belonged. I was too dangerous to be near humans, but not quite Vaettir either. I might share their blood, but I was something entirely foreign to them.

"No," I argued, despite my doubts. "My energy was reborn here for a reason."

"To fill the void I left," she hissed, "nothing more. Leave now, and your loved ones will not be harmed. I swear it. You and your child may live safely in my realm. I will use the well's power to destroy Yggdrasil, and you and I will both be safe from the gods forever."

My stomach twisted at the mention of my loved ones. She was yet to kill them all. Would she truly keep her word if I left voluntarily? My palms began to sweat, adding to the stickiness I already felt from the damp cave.

"Won't the same thing happen again if you destroy the tree?" I questioned, grasping for time. "Won't you be cast out again?"

Her lip curled up into a sneer. "Not *this* time. The tree you created is not like the original Yggdrasil. It does not maintain balance. That's why wild magics are leaking into this world. The original Yggdrasil would not have allowed such a thing to take place."

I blinked at her. "So you really just want me gone so you don't have to share energy with me? Are you *that* power hungry?"

She tilted her head. "I am not power hungry. I simply refuse to lessen myself for all of eternity. I will not have you live here, only to be reborn."

"What will you do if I refuse to go?" I blurted as a sudden thought hit me. She couldn't just kill me, because my energy would be reborn somewhere else, keeping things off balance for her. She needed me to agree to go back.

She took a step forward. "I had hoped you would leave willingly, but if not, you will leave all the same."

I remembered how easily she'd disappeared with her handmaidens when we'd confronted them, and took a step back. It seemed like she hadn't accessed the well's power yet, but could I risk it? If she managed to grab me, could she transport me all the way back to her realm?

"Wait," I hissed, holding my hands up and taking a step back. "I wouldn't send me away just yet. Not if you don't want the gods to come down here themselves."

"What do you know of the gods?" she growled. "Loki does not speak for them all. If he told you—"

I shook my head, wiping a damp strand of dark hair out of my face. My leather coat felt slick with moisture. "It wasn't Loki. Odin told me himself that if you remained here, extreme measures would be taken."

She tilted her head at me. "How did *you* meet the All-Father?"

"He's been watching," I explained. "He knows what you're up to. I'm definitely not your biggest problem." If I could just distract her from the well for even a few minutes...

"Liar," Hecate hissed. "Odin cares not for this realm."

I shrugged. "Don't believe me then. You'll wish you would have listened when he takes the well."

Her green eyes practically bulged out of her head. "He cannot. I need it to—" she cut herself off.

"To what?" I questioned, wishing Silver would hurry up and rouse himself if he yet still breathed. I needed a distraction.

"Nevermind," she growled, taking another step forward. "Come with me."

She was close enough to reach out and touch me. I needed to act *now*. I closed my eyes and reached for the only power available to me. The power of all those Hecate had killed. It was only human energy, not as strong as that of the Vaettir, but there were so many bodies. So much life wasted.

"Don't you dare," Hecate snapped.

I felt a tug on the energy and opened my eyes. Hecate's face was still. I would have guessed she was sleeping standing up if I couldn't feel her sucking in the energy from the dead she'd left above ground.

Acting upon the distraction while I could, I said a silent prayer for Silver, then darted around Hecate for the well. Quickly noticing me, she whirled around just as my hands clamped down on the bronze rim of the cauldron.

The thrumming energy I'd sensed intensified, but it

was nothing I could use. It wasn't the type of energy I was familiar with.

The next thing I knew, Hecate was crouched beside me. She put a hand on my wrist and tugged, but I refused to release my grip on the cauldron's rim.

"You don't know what you're doing," she argued. "Get away from there."

I turned wide eyes to her, surprised she wasn't tugging me away more forcefully, or transporting me back to Yggdrasil. Had she truly not yet taken the well's power? Was she still in a state of sharing energy with me in this realm?

With a defiant smirk, I removed the hand she wasn't tugging on and stuck it into the light emanating from the center of the cauldron. I wasn't sure what would happen, but if I could get to that power before Hecate...

"That won't work," she sighed. "The well is not fully in this realm. *Neither* of us can access its energy when we are not at full power. That is why you must leave this realm."

So she couldn't access it either? It was the best news I'd heard all day.

"Well in that case," I began, then cocked back my free hand and punched her in the jaw.

It was an awkward punch using my left hand while crouched down, but it was enough to rock her head back and loosen her grip on my wrist. Unfortunately the momentum tipped me forward into the well. I caught myself before I could topple all the way head first into the basin.

"How dare you!" Hecate gasped, but her voice was distant.

My face was engulfed in the gentle light of the well. It seeped into me, making my belly grow warm. I realized with a start that the energy was somehow being drawn toward my baby, toward Erykah, and managed to pull myself back out of the well.

"You would dare hit a goddess?" Hecate asked, staring down at me.

I stood, unsure of what had just happened to me. I reached for the long blade down my back and withdrew it, careful not to slice off my braid. "Add it to the list of things I probably shouldn't have done," I quipped, stepping forward with the blade outstretched at my side.

Despite my external confidence, my stomach was quaking and my palms were sweating so much I could barely hold onto the narrow sword's grip. What had the well just done to my baby?

I didn't feel well enough to fight, but if Hecate didn't have the power here to squash me like a bug, I needed to end this before she became strong enough to kill everyone I loved.

I stepped toward her with my blade, then nearly staggered as the energy around us lurched. Cool death energy shifted through the space, flooding toward Hecate.

"Our energy may be shared," she stated, "but I am a *goddess*. You are merely a mortal remnant of Yggdrasil."

Suddenly the energy she'd been sucking in shot outward. It hit me, but rather than knocking me down, it flowed through me.

I exhaled in relief, then smiled. "You may be a goddess, but you and I are cut from the same cloth. Death energy is as much mine as it is yours."

She snarled, then flicked her hand toward the stone ceiling above us. I sensed the power as it shot over my head, then instinctively threw myself to the side as a massive chunk of stone fell down right where I had stood. My shoulder hit the damp ground, making a sickening pop that sent a jolt of pain through my spine. I cradled my belly awkwardly, trying to sit up while searching for the sword that had clattered from my grasp.

When I finally blinked upward, tears of pain creeping out of my eyes, Hecate stood over me. She smirked. "We may be able to access the same energies, but only *I* know how to use them."

My eyes widened a moment before a shovel slammed into Hecate's head. She dropped like a sack of rocks to the ground beside me. I stared at her in shock for a moment, then turned my eyes upward to the culprit.

Alaric.

Behind him stood Faas and Sophie.

"I *told* you I sensed her energy," Faas chided. "She's not trapped in another realm after all."

"What the hell are you doing here!" I cried.

"We could ask you the same question," Faas quipped as Alaric dropped his shovel and fell to his knees in front of me.

He reached out a hand to hover over my shoulder. "You're hurt," he muttered, looking over the rest of my body.

I shook my head and with my uninjured arm scooted away from him. "You can't be here. You're changing the future!"

He narrowed his gaze at me, confused.

"You already know time travel is possible," I blurted, wanting to explain things as quickly as possible. Maybe there was still time for him to go back and not upset the future *too* much. "Well I did that," I continued as Alaric, Sophie, and Faas all stared at me. "The current time Madeline is trapped in Hecate's realm. I'm the future Madeline. Odin sent me back to stop Hecate. If I screw this up, we're all dead!"

Alaric rocked back on his heels, stunned. "I know there's no way you could be here. We came straight from Yggdrasil to this place, only stopping for a moment to drop Aila off at the end of the driveway. So, I know you could not have made it here before us, but . . . " he trailed off, clearly having trouble comprehending my story.

Hecate groaned beside him, beginning to come to.

I struggled to my feet, clutching my injured arm against my chest. I had a feeling my shoulder was dislocated, but I wasn't strong enough to pop it back into place myself. I needed to kill Hecate, but I needed everyone else to get out and go back home. If Alaric wasn't at the house to meet Freyja, would it change us gaining her as an ally?

Sophie stepped around Alaric, grabbed my shoulder, then popped it back into place.

I screamed, and would have fallen if she didn't stabilize me with her sturdy arms.

"There," she said calmly, releasing me and stepping back. "Now, if you truly are from the future, which I believe judging by your horribly dated outfit, and Faas has changed the past in leading us to you, the damage is already done."

Faas muttered angrily under his breath, but didn't argue.

"So the sensible thing to do is deal with Hecate," she continued, "and hope for the best." She turned to look down at the goddess, her gown tangled around her bare legs as she groaned on the floor, seemingly unable to regain full consciousness just yet.

My mind raced for the right answer, but nothing came. It seemed like Odin wanted me to kill her, but that might release her energy into the world, which might take my place. Would I no longer belong if I killed her? I had no idea what the best path would be now that I'd not only changed the past for Silver, but for *everyone* else.

"Find something to bind her arms," I ordered, then

lifted my gaze to Faas. "Do you think you can drain her energy?"

He blinked at me, astonished. "Drain the energy of a *goddess*?"

I nodded. "She's weakened in this realm because I'm here too. We need to get back to the house and find Freyja. She'll know what to do."

"*Freyja*?" Sophie, Alaric, and Faas all balked together.

"Yes," I muttered, searching around for something to bind Hecate's hands since no one else was moving to help. "She should be at the house by now with Aila."

I knew from what little Alaric had told me previously that Freyja had been drawn to the house by Aila's energy, so she was probably with her now. If they'd dropped Aila off on their way, they'd likely just missed her.

Finally Alaric snapped into action and removed his belt, then knelt to begin binding Hecate's arms behind her back.

Faas knelt beside him, placing his hand on Hecate's back. "I can keep her weakened for a time," he explained, "...I think."

"Good," I replied, slowly flexing my fingers to make sure my arm was in working order. It still hurt like hell, but seemed like it would be alright.

As he drained Hecate's energy, Faas looked up at me. "Something is different," he observed. He stood and placed a hand on my belly.

I flicked my gaze to the well. "I might have touched

the big cauldron of magic," I admitted. "Did it do something to Erykah?"

He shook his head. "Her energy feels the same, there's just *more* of it." He turned his attention to the well, dropping his hand from my belly.

"It *is* the same," he gasped. He walked toward it and lowered himself to a crouch. "This energy feels just like Erykah's. What is this thing?"

"It's the Well of Urd," I explained, glancing nervously down at Hecate.

Alaric moved to my side. "Strange wells aside, if we are limited on time, we should probably go."

I nodded, my mind snapping back into action. While Faas continued to observe the well, I hurried over to where Silver lay, then gasped as he blinked up at me. Recovering, I frowned. "You were conscious the entire time, weren't you?"

He scraped his shoulders across the ground in a horizontal shrug. "I was rendered unconscious by Hecate momentarily. Once I awoke, I realized that if the goddess wished to kill you, there was nothing I could have done to stop it. There was no reason to risk my life as well."

Suddenly I felt rage prickling up my back. I turned to see Alaric hovering over me, glaring down at Silver. "She could have been *killed*," he growled.

Silver sat up, shrugging off Alaric's words. "I am not of your clan. She is not my Doyen. You should be grateful I risked myself at all."

I turned toward Alaric. Lifting my good arm, I gently

grabbed his bare bicep. "Don't blame him. He was very clear with me how far he was willing to go to protect me."

His expression softened, but only minutely.

"Now we need to get in a vehicle and get back to the house," I continued. "We only have until tomorrow morning to figure this out."

"What happens tomorrow morning?" Faas asked as he moved back toward Hecate and hefted her over his bony shoulder. The goddess was once again fully unconscious. Faas had done his job thoroughly.

I met Alaric's gaze as I replied, "The me from the present will return to this realm with Mikael and Loki, and things will get *real* weird."

"Lovely," Faas muttered sarcastically, walking past us to carry Hecate out of the cavern.

The rest of us followed, though Silver kept his distance from Alaric. I didn't blame him. I could still feel Alaric's anger like a hot poker being dragged across my skin. Underneath the anger was fear and confusion, and I couldn't help dwelling on the fact that those emotions wouldn't be improving once the present day me returned and admitted she'd made out with another man.

14

It didn't take long to escape the murky cavern and return to where my truck had been parked, right behind Silver's sports car. I'd filled everyone in on my little adventure with the gods, if only to distract myself from all the corpses we passed. There were no police to be seen, which left me wondering just how much carnage had occurred. How many more were dead around the city for it to be so silent? I hadn't forgotten what Odin had said about Hecate placing the city within a bubble of power, but I wasn't sure if that had only happened in the other timeline, or if Hillsboro was somehow cut off from the outside world even now. Whatever the case, it didn't seem to prevent people from leaving or coming in.

As we climbed into the truck, and Silver into his car, a sick knot formed in my stomach and refused to let up. Even if I was changing the past enough to stop Hecate from killing everyone I loved, so many others had died, innocent humans who had nothing to do with the chaotic, violent world of the Vaettir.

I sat in the front passenger seat, not feeling well enough to drive. Alaric assumed the wheel while Sophie and Faas sandwiched Hecate's limp body in the back seats, keeping a close eye on her.

Alaric started the ignition, backed up, then turned the truck to drive back toward the house, all the while keeping his free hand on my leg, as if afraid I might disappear.

"If all you say is true," Faas began, leaning forward from the backseat, "then why don't we just kill Hecate while we can?"

I turned to see him glance at her, then shook my head. "Trust me, I considered it, and if I'd had no other choice, I would have. The only issue is I'm not quite sure what killing her would do. When I returned to this realm, which I'll be doing tomorrow, we had learned that Hecate would need to utterly obliterate my energy in order to exist here at full power. That was why she had trapped me in her realm. If we kill her, if we even *can* kill her, her energy might be released here too, then I might no longer belong. I really don't want to give the gods any reason to kill me."

"But you *do* belong here," Alaric argued, keeping his eyes on the road.

I sighed. "Yes, but technically, so does Hecate. I just want to speak with Freyja before we do anything that might upset the balance of this realm, hence making the gods none too happy with me."

His eyes on the road, Alaric shook his head, an expression of disbelief on his face. "I still can't believe you ventured to the realm of the gods."

"Tell me about it," I replied, placing my hand on top of his where it rested on my leg.

"And where was I when you were taken there?" he asked.

My gut clenched painfully. I'd tactfully avoided that part. How do you tell someone that in your timeline, they're dead? My gaze flicked to Sophie in the rearview mirror. They were *all* dead. I fought the urge to vomit. I wasn't sure what was going to happen to me when all was said and done, but at least my loved ones now had a chance of survival.

"Madeline?" he pressed when I didn't answer.

I squeezed his hand. "I'll tell you when all of this is over, I promise."

He took me at my word, and we continued the drive in silence. I had royally screwed things up by changing everyone's pasts, but hopefully Freyja would be willing to help. In this timeline, she hadn't yet met me, but I'd be handing her Hecate on a silver platter, so maybe she'd be willing to believe my wild tale, and maybe, just maybe, there was hope for us all yet.

WHEN WE REACHED THE HOUSE, the knot still hadn't left my gut, and I started to wonder if something was wrong with me physically . . . besides the scrapes and bruises provided by Hecate. My thoughts darted back to the light from the well, and Faas' observations. Could a little extra energy hurt my child?

There was no time for my thoughts to linger on the worst case scenario as we pulled up to the dimly lit house. Our headlights illuminated several figures standing near the front door. I immediately recognized Freyja, and struggled to quickly release my seatbelt and stumble out of the truck just as the vehicle came to a slow stop.

Freyja and Aila both whipped their gazes to me as I approached. Further back were Alejandro and Frode, both looking like they had their hackles up about something.

Freyja watched me curiously for a moment as I walked toward her, then balked at something behind me. I stopped walking and turned to see Sophie and Faas lugging Hecate out of the truck. Alaric came to stand by my side.

"How did this happen?" Freyja gasped.

I turned back toward her. "This may be hard to believe, but you actually know me. The you in the future just sent me down Yggdrasil's branch from the realm of the gods."

She stopped her approach toward Hecate, finally

turning to fully regard me. "That's absurd. Time travel is forbidden."

I shrugged. "So is letting Hecate use the Well of Urd. Odin sent me back in lieu of severing the World Tree branch in your realm."

"Odin?" Freyja hissed, echoed by Aila.

I nodded. "Yes, and we have limited time. So I need you to tell me what to do with Hecate now that we have her. She and I share the same energy. Will killing her release too much of said energy into this realm? Can we take her back to her realm and maybe trap her there?"

Freyja blinked her shimmering blue eyes at me, then quickly recovered her cool demeanor. "Who are you, and why should I believe your insane story?"

"This would be so much easier if Loki was here," I muttered, grasping for a way to make her quickly believe me.

"Loki?" she questioned. "Where is that little weasel? He's the reason I'm here to begin with."

I sighed. "He's in Hecate's realm, waiting to help the present day me to escape with Mikael. I need you to trust that I know what I'm talking about. The present day me will return to this realm in the morning, and I don't know what will happen."

She pursed her full lips and looked me up and down. "Well you *do* share Hecate's energy. Let us continue this conversation over a meal, and then I shall decide whether or not I believe you." She turned to Aila expectantly.

"Yes!" Aila blurted. "Please come inside." She gestured toward the front door.

"Finally," Freyja said, rolling her eyes. "I had begun to think your people would question me until I starved."

She turned away from us as Aila explained that I was Doyen of their clan, so my trust outweighed any suspicion on the part of the others.

I rolled my eyes and followed, with Alaric and the others trailing close behind. It was funny how little nuances within the same timeline could differ, like Freyja being forced to wait outside rather than being directly invited in.

There was only one thing that seemed to stay consistent throughout all timelines: the gods were always hungry.

Ten minutes later, Freyja was scraping the remnants of chili from her bowl, and mulling over all I had told her. Hecate was tied to a chair beside us at the dining table, her energy continually drained by Faas as a precaution. However, now that we had Freyja on our side, and Hecate was at a low power level from sharing energy with me, I wasn't as worried about her waking up. In fact, it might be a good thing. She might be willing to make a deal with us that would allow things to go back to normal.

Alaric, Sophie, and Faas all sat around the table in

the seats nearest to me. They remained silent through my explanation, likely still trying to believe the elaborate tale themselves.

"Now," Freyja began, sucking her spoon clean, "tell me again exactly what Odin ordered you to do."

I sighed, glancing at the clock on the adjacent wall. The night was only just beginning, but I couldn't help being anxious about wasting what precious time we had.

"I was supposed to prevent Hecate from using the well," I explained. "Which," I gestured to Hecate tied up in her chair, "I did. Now I just need to figure out what to do with her."

Freyja stared at Hecate for several seconds. "Fine. I suppose it does not matter if I believe you when it comes to her. She must be placed back in her realm, and the branch of the World Tree that allowed her to escape must be severed."

"Thank you," I sighed, close to exasperation. I winced at a pang in my belly.

"What is it?" Alaric asked, carefully watching my face.

I cringed, leaning forward, but the pain would not abate. "I don't know," I rasped. "I thought it was just nerves, but maybe something is wrong."

"*Faas*," Alaric said sharply, summoning him from his chair.

Flipping his white-blond hair out of his face, Faas hurried to my side, then placed his palm against my belly. I watched as he closed his eyes, sensing my energy, and that of the baby.

The pain became like a second heartbeat, reverberating through my abdomen and down my legs. I began to feel lightheaded. I felt Alaric stroking my hair, then the world went black.

I WOKE up to sharp pain lancing through my insides. I was in an oddly familiar bed. Fluffy white pillows surrounded me and a fire was crackling in the nearby hearth, chasing away the darkness.

A sudden jolt of pain wracked my entire body, lifting me from the bed. I forced my eyes open as hands pressed down on my shoulders. "She's awake!" Alaric's voice called.

Faas' face came into view, then Sophie's, then . . . Sif's? What the hell was I doing back in the realm of the gods?

"Out of my way," Sif demanded, her golden hair shimmering in the firelight. Sweat glistened on her plump cheeks, as if she'd been running before I awoke. Without warning, she lifted up the bottom edge of my blanket, along with the hem of the nightgown someone had put me in.

"What the hell!" I gasped.

Alaric sat by my side and leaned over to cradle my head, rubbing his hands up and down my biceps. "It's okay," he soothed. "We think the baby might be coming."

"But it's not time!" I shouted in his face. "You people are crazy!" I continued, my gaze darting frantically around the room. "It's dangerous to have a baby this early!"

"You are not human, Madeline," Alaric said softly.

The bed shifted on my other side as someone sat. I turned to see Sophie.

"It's okay, Maddy," she soothed. "We're all here."

I shook my head, trying to shove away my terror and confusion. This wasn't right. Not only could I not have a baby right now, but what about the me that would soon be returning from Hecate's realm? Would she arrive only to find Alaric and Sophie missing?

"You guys have to go back to our realm," I managed to grunt through the pain. "When present day Maddy returns, there won't be anyone there to meet her."

"You are present day Madeline," a voice said somewhere behind Sif's back. She'd luckily let the blankets fall back down to cover me.

I relaxed just an iota as Freyja stepped forward to where I could see her. "When I brought you back through Yggdrasil, you were brought back into the proper timeline for your present day self. You've already gone to Hecate's realm and come back."

I looked around the room frantically. "If that's the case, then where is Mikael?"

I whipped my head to the side in time to see Alaric's

frown, and suddenly I knew they were telling me the truth. I'd come back from Hecate's realm and told Alaric about mine and Mikael's kiss.

"If I'm the present day me," I began between pants, "then why the hell am I having my baby?"

Freyja sighed. "The past you and present you are the same people, so what you did to stop Hecate still happened. Just think of it as you having experienced this for twelve hours, bringing you up to the present time, only twelve hours haven't passed."

I shook my head, gritting my jaw against the pain. "So I still went to Hecate's realm, but I also didn't go, because I was in my realm? Then what about Mikael? He was only in one place during that time. He's still in that place in this time!"

"Don't worry about your Viking friend," she replied. "The Loki that was here to send you to Yggdrasil fetched him from the present that was present to you, after you changed the past to prevent his death. Time tends to balance itself out when it can. Your companions are now missing a short length of time in their timelines, but it should be inconsequential to their continued existence."

My brain began to ache almost as much as the rest of me. If I was the present me in a present time, and Loki had retrieved Mikael from the new present, that had to mean . . .

"So I officially saved them?" I gasped, darting my gaze back to Freyja. "It worked? Hecate didn't kill them on any timeline?"

She nodded, a small smile playing across her lips. "Well she killed them in one timeline, but that timeline is no longer your reality. You have a bit of a dual reality now, with being in two places at once, but since it was such a short span of time it shouldn't affect you too much. Hecate is here, for now. She will be awarded a trial, after which she will ultimately be banished. Mikael is with Loki . . . *discussing* things with Odin."

I would have been relieved if I didn't feel the sudden urge to vomit. Anther wave of pain took over, making the corners of my vision turn white.

Sif lifted the blanket again, and this time I didn't have the strength to fight her. "It's time," she said.

"No, no, *no*," I said over and over again. I wasn't prepared for this. I was still supposed to have plenty of time.

Someone placed a hand on my forehead, and cool energy washed over me. *Death* energy.

I opened my eyes to see Faas sitting by Sophie, his hand stretched to my forehead. "Do not be afraid, Madeline," he said softly. "I will help replenish the energy you have lost. You are ready for this."

I nodded, though I didn't believe him. I turned my gaze to Alaric, who smiled down at me as he took my hand, giving it a squeeze.

I closed my eyes as my body convulsed, and gave in to the fact that this was happening. I was about to have my baby in the realm of the gods, while Mikael and Loki were likely bargaining with Odin for the sake of us all.

Leave it to me to screw up something as natural and uncomplicated as giving birth.

"*Breathe*," Sif instructed, glancing up from her post at the foot of the bed.

My blanket and nightgown had been thrown up, leaving my lower region bare to the room. Though a bit embarrassed, the upcoming contraction cancelled my modesty. I was grateful only Faas, Sophie, Alaric, and Sif were in the room, though I would have preferred a hospital with an actual doctor. Freyja had left us at least, feeling she should not be part of the intimate moment.

Another contraction wracked my body, and Faas pressed down more firmly on my forehead, soothing me with his energy. Sandwiched against my other side, Alaric clutched my hand. Sophie had stepped back toward the head of the bed. I could sense her discomfort like a small gnat buzzing around the back of my skull, but she refused to leave the room.

I cried out as the pain stabbed me like a thousand knives. "Is this how it's supposed to feel?" I panted. "It feels like something is wrong."

"Your baby is highly magical," Sif explained calmly. "She is coming now because your body became too weak, and could no longer contain her power."

I wanted more information, but the pain hit me again. Another contraction, stronger than the previous. I could barely feel Faas' soothing energy now. Another contraction hit me.

"She's coming!" Sif said excitedly.

Alaric squeezed my hand and leaned forward to see. I tried to watch him through the stars clouding my vision, then finally had to shut my eyes. Contraction after contraction hit me as my body naturally began to push out the baby. I'd heard horrible tales of twenty hour long labor, but apparently Erykah wanted out *now*. At least there was that.

I screamed again through the pain.

"Just a little more!" Sif encouraged.

I screamed again, then pushed, and suddenly I could hear a baby crying, though it sounded distant, like I was in a dream. I heard splashing water with continued crying.

Alaric stroked sweaty strands of hair back from my face, his gaze flicking between me and Sif, who was tending the baby. My heart ached with anticipation. I *needed* to hold her. Finally, Sif walked around the bed. Blood and other fluids stained the white sleeves of her dress, and in her arms she held a small form, swaddled in a cream colored cloth.

My heart exploded as she set Erykah in my arms. I looked down at the now calm baby. I was completely enamored.

Alaric leaned back and put an arm around my shoulders, cradling us both with adoration. I couldn't believe it had all happened so quickly. I couldn't believe she was actually in my arms, *real*.

Sophie and Faas both hovered over us as Sif backed away.

Sophie reached out and gently stroked Erykah's reddish cheek. "I know a first name has already been chosen," she crooned, "but I strongly suggest a *strong* middle name like Sophie."

"I'll consider it," I whispered, my eyes glued to my child.

The firelight flickered off the gray of her half-closed eyes, and her sparse shock of black hair. She blinked up at me, unbelievably calm, and I couldn't help but feel like I held an age-old being in my arms. Her magic pulsed against my chest.

Alaric stared down at her in awe. "Can you feel her magic?" he muttered. "How did we create something so . . . light?"

I nodded, tears of happiness in my eyes. Though I'd come to terms with my death energy, and no longer thought of it as evil, it had also caused me so much struggle. I hadn't wanted my daughter to go through that. I still didn't know just how she'd turn out, but the energy I sensed from her was nothing like mine. It felt like the first kiss of sunshine on a calm, babbling brook, while mine was the pale shadows cast by the moon.

"She's perfect," I whispered, leaning down to kiss her forehead.

Her eyes had fluttered closed, and she seemed fast asleep.

Alaric pulled me closer, while Sophie and Faas made themselves comfortable at the foot of the bed, silently watching the three of us.

We were still trapped in the realm of the gods with many obstacles before us, but in that moment, I reveled in the feeling of family. It was a feeling I'd never thought to have, but I'd somehow found it in spades.

MIKAEL GLARED up at the All-Father, sitting up on his dais, lording over him and Loki. He'd always felt great reverence for the gods, but this one...well, he was kind of a prick.

"You've completely changed the past and allowed wild magics to continue flowing into Midgard," Odin growled, his pale eyes narrowed into angry slits. "Now you expect the gods to further aid you?"

Loki bowed his head respectfully. "What Mikael is trying to say, is that if you would so graciously allow him, perhaps he could still fix things. Madeline *did* prevent Hecate from using the well, as promised, and even took her prisoner."

"Yes," Odin hissed, "and you brought her here to disrupt *our* realm. The sooner we execute her and send her energy back down Yggdrasil, the better."

"Of course," Loki agreed. "And the sooner we send

the Vaettir back to fix the disaster in their realm, the better."

Odin scowled. "We must first decide what to do with the child."

"The child?" Mikael balked. "She has already arrived?"

Odin inclined his head.

Mikael wasn't sure how Odin had known when the baby was born, none of them had left the room, but it didn't matter.

"If you'll excuse me," he bowed his head, concealing the emotions within him. He knew Erykah was not his child, but he couldn't help feeling almost as excited as he had when his own daughter was born, many centuries ago. Now, he needed to see Madeline. He needed to—

He waited as Odin glared down at him, then finally nodded his head. "You are dismissed. Be prepared for Hecate's trial in the morning. We will settle the rest of our business after that."

He practically ran from the room while Loki stayed behind with Odin.

As soon as the door shut behind him, he fled down the hall, retracing the steps he'd taken earlier when he'd been forced to leave Madeline and the others behind. Odin had wanted an audience with the Doyen of their clan, and with Madeline unconscious, that only left Mikael.

Reaching the door to Madeline's room, he paused with his hand on the doorknob. What was he doing? He would not be welcome at the birth of Madeline's child, not after his foolish actions in Hecate's realm.

He let his hand drop from the door, then took a step back as it opened to reveal Sophie.

Excitement glinted in her dark eyes. "Her middle name is Sophie." She grinned.

"We haven't decided that yet!" Madeline's voice called from within the room, though with the angle of the door, he could not see her.

"I just wanted to make sure everything was alright," he lied. "I'll leave you to your celebration."

Sophie's lip twitched in annoyance. "What are you talking about, idiot? Don't you want to meet Erykah?"

"Is that Mikael?" Madeline called out, echoed by the gentle sound of a baby cooing.

His heart swelled.

Sophie grabbed his sleeve and tugged him into the room. "Hurry up before the gods come barging in."

He stumbled into the room. He felt dizzy. He wasn't quite sure what was wrong with him. He *never* stumbled.

Fighting through the fog in his mind, he lifted his gaze to the bed. In the middle sat Madeline, propped against several white fluffy pillows. Her face was marred with exhaustion, but beneath the puffy eyes and the tired droop of her shoulders, she glowed.

On either side of her sat Faas and Alaric. Faas crooked his finger at the baby while making stupid noises. Alaric watched Mikael cautiously.

To his surprise, Alaric nodded, then stood and stepped aside for Mikael to approach.

"Thank you," Mikael muttered as he passed him.

Alaric shook his head. "She wanted you to meet Erykah."

Mikael wasn't quite able to focus on Alaric as he looked down at the small shape in Madeline's arms.

"Do you want to hold her?" she asked. She nodded to Alaric's vacated seat.

Mikael quickly sat down, then Madeline extended Erykah to him. He took the small child in his arms. She was so tiny. It had been many years since he'd bothered with holding a child.

He stared down at her in awe. The baby blinked up at him, her eyes a murky stone color that could easily turn into pure gray, or blue like her mother's. The light swath of hair on her head was black, no surprise with both her parents having dark hair.

He lifted his eyes to find Madeline smiling at him.

He didn't know why he said what he said next, the words simply spewed forth from his mouth. "I will protect her as long as I am alive."

Madeline laughed. "I know."

Alaric moved to stand at Mikael's side, smiling down at his daughter.

In his many lifetimes, Mikael was quite sure he'd never felt as close to his long-lost home as he did in that moment.

15

I was barely able to sleep during the night, especially since *everyone* insisted on sleeping in my room. Sophie and Alaric lay on either side of me as the first rays of sunlight crept through the gauzy curtains.

Mikael was on the chaise near said windows, leaving Faas to sleep on some blankets on the floor.

Erykah was nestled in the crook of my arm. I'd been afraid to sleep with her, but Alaric had assured me I wouldn't crush her.

I gazed down at her sleeping face. I *never* wanted to get out of bed, but Hecate's trial was to be that morning, and I needed to be there.

My body was sore, but Sif had returned to tend to me, and I had a feeling I was doing far better than I should have been. Perhaps the gods were good for *some* things.

I labored to sit up slowly with Erykah cradled in my

arms. Sophie groaned in irritation, but Alaric was instantly awake, helping me scoot myself up against the pillows.

Erykah awoke and peered up at us both, her deep gray eyes bleary.

"She doesn't cry much," Alaric whispered, smiling down at her.

I shook my head. "No, she doesn't."

I was actually a little uneasy about how little she'd cried so far, she was so calm, and seemed oddly observant for a newborn.

I pulled the loose neck of my nightgown down, and lifted Erykah to feed her, the movement not yet natural to me.

Alaric extended his far arm to help me, cradling Erykah in place while I adjusted to a better position. I jumped as she clamped on, then relaxed.

"Maddy," Alaric began softly, "I'd like to speak with you."

My stomach did a nervous little flip as I looked up to him. "Are you sure now is the time?"

He nodded, then keeping his voice low, explained, "I need to apologize."

My eyes widened. "*What*?"

He smiled ruefully. "I should have listened to you before. You are entitled to your feelings. That you are five centuries younger than me does not counteract the fact that you are wise beyond your years."

I smirked. "I'm really not. In fact, I'm an utter fool half the time."

He shook his head. "Perhaps you are sometimes naive, but in your heart, you know many things that I have yet to learn. I should not have been surprised that you had developed feelings for Mikael. He has stayed by your side at times when I could not. He loves you."

I squirmed and dropped my chin, feeling suddenly uncomfortable.

He placed a finger under my chin and brought my eyes back up to his. "You, Erykah, and Sophie are the only things that matter to me in this world, but I know I cannot protect you alone. As much as I hate Mikael, I would not send him away, even if I could. If I fail to keep you safe, I know he will be there to catch you."

"Alaric," I began softly, fighting tears. "I don't even know what I feel. The only thing I know for sure is that I love *you*."

He nodded. "I know, and I love you. I just want to let you know that you do not have to worry. I will be by your side as long as you will have me, and I cannot wait for us to raise Erykah together."

"You know," I began with a small smile, "most men would have kicked me to the curb and called it a day."

He winked at me through the strands of black hair that had fallen into his face. "I am not most men."

I snuggled into the crook of his arm as Erykah relinquished her hold on me and fell back to sleep. Soon the others awoke, and we all prepared for the trial to come, though we weren't sure what to expect.

The gods now held Hecate's fate in the palms of their hands. I could only hope she received the punishment she deserved.

I WASN'T sure what I'd been expecting from the court-room of the gods, but whatever I might have envisioned could not do it justice. Ivory pillars extended toward an impossibly high ceiling along the border of the room, accenting marble walls etched with what appeared to be real gold inlaid with crystals.

The blue velvet cushioned seats at the back end of the room were filled with men and women that I had to assume were other gods, all facing the open front portion of the room, dominated by a marble podium depicting three Norns. Before the podium were two separate tables with seats behind them, like in a standard courtroom, only the tables were made of heavy, gleaming wood and the seats were embroidered with gold thread depicting flowers and leaves. No one yet stood behind the marble podium facing the room, but in a little seat below it was Hecate, her entire body wrapped in chains that had to weigh over a hundred pounds.

The ornate room made me feel woefully under-dressed, the loose lavender dress provided by Sif pooling around my ankles as I walked down the cushy carpeting in my simple flats. Mikael walked beside me, entirely unashamed of his suede pants and black tee-shirt. We were escorted down the center of the room and instructed to sit in two of the embroidered seats behind the table on the right.

As we sat, Loki and Freyja entered the room, Freyja in a flowing silver dress with blue jewels cinching the sleeveless shoulders, and Loki in a purple linen tunic embroidered with gold, striking against his black pants. They walked through the aisles of those already seated, then took the two remaining chairs at our table, leaving me sandwiched between Loki and Mikael.

Entering the room next were several more gods I didn't recognize, though I suspected the muscly blond one might be Thor. They made their way to the other table adjacent ours.

Everyone muttered amongst themselves, no one speaking to Hecate.

Loki leaned in toward my shoulder. "I doubt you'll be asked to speak much, except to vote on the final judgement."

"Final judgement?" I questioned softly, glancing warily around the room. I was glad I'd left Erykah with Alaric, Sophie, and Faas. I would have hated bringing her into this room full of imposing gods.

Loki nodded. "Her crimes will be stated, then those of us who have been appointed to the vote for this trial will decide Hecate's fate. Mikael will not be given a vote, but the three of us will," he gestured between me, him, and Freyja, "along with those chosen at random to participate," he gestured to the four seated at the other table. "Normally the vote is eight, with Odin to decide the final fate, but today it will be seven, as Mikael's presence was requested as Co-Doyen of your clan."

I nodded, feeling numb. I couldn't take my eyes off Hecate, wondering if I were truly worthy of passing judgement on her. She'd murdered countless humans to unearth the well, and in another timeline, had murdered everyone I loved, but it was still uncomfortable to pass judgement on her. She seemed so small, weighed down by the chains atop her dirty white dress, the same one she'd been wearing when I confronted her. She turned, as if sensing my gaze. Her green eyes stared at me for several seconds, *accusing*, then she turned back around.

The din of conversation in the room abruptly silenced. I looked over my shoulder to see Odin striding in from the back of the room. He wore the black robes of a judge, though to me he looked like a grizzled wizard... not that I'd say it to his face.

He walked down the aisle as all gazed on reverently. He passed our table, then ascended the stairs positioned behind the ornate podium. Once at the top, facing the room, he swung an delicately carved gavel against the podium's marble surface, calling the room to order.

Loki leaned toward my shoulder again. "Now comes the naming of Hecate's crimes," he whispered. "It's a long list."

With no flourish or introduction, Odin glared down

at Hecate. "Goddess Hecate," he began, "you stand before the court a goddess disgraced. Your list of crimes is long, therefore I will name only the chief amongst them. You are the destroyer of Yggdrasil. You evaded banishment decreed by the gods. You returned to the realm from which you were banished, and attempted to use the Well of Urd..."

The list went on and on, though he neglected to mention she actually *did* use the Well of Urd. I supposed now with the alteration in the timeline, it hadn't actually happened, though I was pretty sure a timeline still existed where it did. He also forgot to mention the countless humans she slaughtered.

When the list was finally done, he asked, "How do you plead?"

Staring at her back, I watched her auburn hair shift as she hung her head. "I see no use in pleading innocent due to circumstance. The Old Gods have never been merciful to me."

"A wise choice," Odin agreed. "Nothing you might say will disprove your actions. It would only waste our time. Now, we will vote on your punishment."

Odin started with the god furthest from us at the left table. The god flicked long, blond hair behind his shoulder and glared at Hecate haughtily. "The guilty party should be put to death," he announced, "and her energy dispersed through Yggdrasil that it may not burden our realm."

The next god, a woman with jet black hair cropped

just below her chin, nodded politely to the first god as he finished his statement. In a voice that sounded like a tinkling wind chime she announced, "I vote for Hecate to be put to death, and her energy disposed of as the All-Father sees fit."

The next two gods made similar statements. All the while, Hecate hung her head, not fighting back. She seemed utterly broken, nothing like the strong, scary woman I'd faced less than twenty-four hours ago.

The vote came to Freyja, sitting with her spine erect at the end of our table. "Hecate must die for her crimes," she agreed. "Madeline has done us a great service in bringing her in for judgement."

I let out a slow breath. I'd have to thank her later for the subtle endorsement. I knew I was still on thin ice with the other gods.

Odin's gaze shifted to Loki as he waited for him to speak next.

Loki rolled his eyes and slouched in his seat. "We already know you're going to kill her, let's just get on with it."

Odin's shoulders lifted, then dropped with a heavy sigh as his one-eyed gaze turned to me.

My palms began to sweat. Unresponsive until now, Hecate shifted in her chair, craning her neck to see me.

My mouth went dry. I couldn't help but feel connected to her in some way. In fact, in many ways, we were the same, but—I flashed on all the bodies leading down to the well, and I remembered how I'd felt when

Loki and Freyja told me everyone I loved was dead. Hecate did not value life as fleeting as what mortals possessed.

"I wish," I began, my voice weak.

Loki nodded to me encouragingly. I could feel Mikael's anxiety pulsing at my other side, but he kept quiet.

"I wish it were simple for me to pass judgement," I began more loudly as the words finally came to me. "Death would be the easy choice, but I do not feel it is justice for all the lives lost. I wish we could go back in time and undo it all." Loki grabbed my leg under the table and squeezed, *hard*.

Odin glared daggers at me. "Choose your words wisely, mortal."

I gulped. "If such things cannot be changed," I quickly added, "if those lives are truly lost, then I can only wish for Hecate to understand just what she has done. I don't know how that could be. The only way she'd truly understand would be for her to be made mortal, to understand that her life holds no more value than anyone else's."

Odin's expression softened, and he tilted his head to the side in thought.

I wasn't sure why though, everyone else had already agreed on a vote.

Suddenly, he smiled. "I like it, a truly creative punishment, and it will save us from the messy process of dispersing her energy. Hecate will be stripped of her magic and of her immortality. She will live out her days in a cell, with an entire human lifetime to repent on what she has done."

My jaw dropped as the room erupted in conversation. I turned to Loki, who was grinning.

"It seems you have made an impression on the All-Father," he whispered. "Normally he just hears the votes then makes up a punishment of his own."

My jaw still agape, I turned to Mikael.

He shrugged, his expression still worried.

"Now on to the next order of business," Odin announced, drawing all eyes to him. His gaze was solely on me as he added, "The trial of Madeline Ville."

The courtroom erupted once again in loud murmurs. I couldn't quite seem to breathe. I knew I had a lot to answer for, but I hadn't expected a trial like Hecate's. A trial where the gods were all too willing to hand out death sentences.

Loki stood abruptly. "A mortal cannot face trial amongst the gods!"

Odin chuckled. "Ah, but she is no mere mortal. Truly, she has a power not unlike any of our half-mortal children. She shall be tried as such."

I began to stand, but Mikael put a hand on my shoulder. "Let Loki do the talking," he whispered.

I nodded subtly, then sat, though it seemed the discussion was over. Everyone in the courtroom muttered amongst themselves.

"On what crimes?" Loki asked more calmly.

Odin smirked. "For the crime of regrowing Yggdrasil on Midgard, releasing wild magics." The murmurs around the room grew louder.

"Fine," Loki sighed as he sat.

I watched as Odin turned to the gods at the left hand table. "Clear away the debris of the previous trial, then resume your seats in the crowd. We will require fresh council."

The blond man and black-haired woman were the first to move. They grabbed the back of Hecate's chair and began dragging it loudly across the courtroom floor toward an exit on the far left.

Hecate began to scream, "You are all fools! The old gods are little more than children! You cannot do this to me!"

Her screams continued as she was dragged out of the room. She never once looked at me as she disappeared from sight.

"Don't worry," Loki comforted as I stared at the now empty doorway. "You haven't really done anything wrong, and you kept your deal to stop Hecate. There are no laws against regrowing Yggdrasil because we thought it could not be done."

I swallowed the lump in my throat, feeling none-too comforted by his words. Hecate's screams still echoed in my ears.

I raised my gaze to Odin, who watched me with a smug expression, as if daring me to argue.

I knew in that moment Odin wanted something from

me. Something beyond capturing Hecate and returning me to my normal life.

My hands trembled underneath the table as I thought of Erykah. I would protect her at all costs, the Old Gods be damned.

SOON ENOUGH I was in a new seat before the podium replacing Hecate, though no chains bound my body. A new panel of gods had been elected to the tables, and Loki, Freyja, and Mikael had been forced back to sit with the crowd. I glanced over my shoulder at them longingly. So much for any votes in my favor.

"Madeline Ville," Odin began, drawing my attention to the marble podium. "You stand before us accused of regrowing Yggdrasil, releasing wild magics into Midgard, traveling to Hecate's realm without permission from the gods, and irreparably changing the past to a point where you have altered the fate of Midgard entirely."

"She *saved* Midgard," Loki interrupted from his place in the crowd, striking up a fresh wave of murmurs.

Odin scowled. "Be that as it may, all of these things are against our age old laws. How do you plead?"

Was he serious? *He* gave me permission to go back and stop Hecate, and Loki took me to Hecate's realm. I had permission for all of it...except maybe regrowing Yggdrasil.

"You know I did those things," I stated boldly,

smoothing the skirt of my lilac gown over my legs, "and you also know what little I did without permission, I had no choice in."

The murmurs began anew. Odin slammed his palm down on the podium. The noise echoed across the large room, immediately cutting off all conversation.

"Since you will not debate you crimes," he said smugly, "we shall vote on your punishment."

I shook my head. These trials moved so fast it was jarring. They weren't really trials at all. Anyone who sat before the podium had already been deemed guilty. "I didn't say I wouldn't debate them!" I blurted. "I said I had permission for most of them! Loki took me to Hecate's realm, and *you* told me I had one day to go back in time and stop Hecate from using the well, *which* I did."

"Yes," Odin agreed blandly. "Then you brought even more mortals into our realm when you returned."

"Enough of this," Loki's voice sounded from behind me, closer than where he'd been sitting.

I turned to see he had vacated his seat to approach us.

He didn't stop until he reached my side and glared up at Odin. "Just tell Madeline what you want from her so we can all get on with our lives."

Odin's eye glittered with mischief, and I knew I wouldn't like whatever he was about to stay.

"As you wish," he replied. "I am reluctant to sever our hold on Midgard now that Hecate has been dealt with, but the land will soon be in utter ruin. Though the well remains unactivated, magics will still be drawn toward it. It's only a matter of time before things get even worse."

Thinking of my world, I bit my lip. All of those Hecate had killed, the wild magics we'd seen in the woods...it was only the beginning as long as Yggdrasil stood.

"You truly cannot expect *her* to do anything about it," Loki gestured down to me.

Odin tilted his head to the side. "She is the reason it has happened, therefore she must clean up her mess."

"What?" I gasped, shaking my head in disbelief. I'd seen the wild magics in the woods, and felt the well's power. "How do you expect me to *clean it up*?"

The room was eerily silent. I could feel the crowd's eagerness and excitement as they waited to hear Odin's final ruling.

"You have two choice's," he began. "We can put your fate to a vote, a vote which will likely end in your death, or you and I can strike a deal."

I glanced to Loki. Would the gods really all vote for my death? I supposed in their eyes, maybe I wasn't much different from Hecate.

"Let her hear your deal," Loki suggested, "then let her decide."

Odin inclined his head. "Very well," he turned his eye to me, "I will offer you one year in which you and your child will reside in our realm. You will be allowed to venture forth with your companions to fix your realm, but your child will remain here to ensure your return."

Suddenly all thoughts of my own survival went out of my head. "I will *not* leave my child here."

He raised the brow above his eyeless socket. "You would rather take her into your realm, where chaos reigns?"

I opened my mouth, then shut it when no words came out. What could I say? Would Erykah truly be safer here?

"If I'm to agree to your deal," I began hesitantly, "it will only be on the condition that some of my people may remain here to care for her when I cannot, and that I will be allowed to return to her every night."

Odin narrowed his one good eye. "So be it. You may choose five companions total to either travel back and forth with you, or stay with the child. You will have one year to save your realm, and if you fail, your child will remain *here* forever."

My jaw dropped as my stomach plummeted. "What are you, the *Goblin King*? I will not give you my child."

"You will have no choice," he countered. "You can choose to let the council decide your fate, which I guarantee you, will be death. If you die today, your child will remain here. *Or*, you can choose to take one year to save your realm. If you succeed, you, your child, and all of your companions may live out your days peacefully in Midgard."

I looked to Loki again, who shrugged. "I'd take the year. At least that way you'll stand a chance."

My heart fluttered in my chest like a caged

hummingbird. *One Year.* A lot could happen in a year. If I couldn't save my realm, it would at least give me time to figure out how to escape Odin, and in the meantime, Erykah would be safe from the wild magics in my world.

"Deal," I breathed, though it felt like my heart was tearing in two. "I'll take the year to save my realm."

Odin's smile turned the blood in my veins to ice. I'd given him exactly what he wanted. I'd had no choice. The only question now was, why did he want it? Why did he want my child?

MIKAEL FUMED like an angry storm at my side as we made our way down the hall back toward the room where Alaric, Sophie, and Faas waited with Erykah.

"We have to escape," he growled. "We can run away to our realm and destroy Yggdrasil."

"That is unwise," Loki replied calmly from my other side. "There are other ways, ways long ago forbidden, to travel between the realms. I have no doubt Odin will break our laws to use them. He will find you."

I could barely focus on their words. All that mattered were my feet moving me forward, slower than I wished as I was still sore from childbirth despite Sif's remedies. My arms yearned to hold my baby to the point where I felt ill. How was I supposed to leave her in this realm every day to go back to my reality without her? Alaric and Sophie wouldn't like it, but I planned on asking them to stay behind with her while I tried to contain the magics in our realm, maybe Faas and Aila too. Mikael would need to stay in our realm to watch over our clan with me having to go back and forth.

Mikael and Loki both fell silent as we reached the door.

I gripped the handle, flung the door open, then rushed inside, my heart in my throat. I had no reason to believe something had happened while I was away, but I couldn't help my worry. I didn't feel safe here, not when the gods could easily decide that none of us should exist.

My shoulders slumped in relief to find Alaric and Sophie sitting side by side on the chaise with their matching black hair and clothing, fawning over Erykah, swaddled in white. They both looked up at me, smiles on their faces.

"What happened?" Alaric asked, his smile faltering.

I shook my head, unsure of where to begin. Fortunately, Mikael stepped in.

"We have one year to fix the magic leak in our realm," he explained. "We will all live here, venturing into our realm each day to work on remedying the problem."

I'd started toward Alaric to take Erykah from him, but Mikael's words gave me pause. I turned toward him. "We can't all live here. What about our clan? I assumed you'd be returning to watch over them, especially with the threat of wild magics on the loose."

He scoffed, a hint of panic in his amber eyes. "I

cannot just leave you and Erykah here unprotected, Madeline."

Alaric got to his feet beside me, a slumbering Erykah still in his arms. "I'd say she *won't* be unprotected, but I'd really like to know what the hell is going on first. How are we supposed to stop the flow of magic into our realm? *Why* are we supposed to stop the flow of magic into our realm?"

I bit my lip as I turned to him. "*I'm* supposed to stop it, and Erykah has to stay here while I do. I want you and Sophie to stay with her. I'll be able to return each night, but during the day..." I shook my head. "I cannot stand the thought of leaving her with anyone else."

"Why do you have to leave her at all?" Sophie demanded, moving to stand beside Alaric. "I don't understand. Isn't everything supposed to be over now? We need to return to our normal lives."

Faas entered the room, a tray of food in his hands. Instantly sensing the vibe, he asked, "What's going on?"

Loki, who'd been waiting quietly by the door, stepped forward. "I believe I can explain."

We all turned to him.

"Odin wants your child," he stated. "I do not know why, but I intend to find out. In the meantime, you must all play along with the deal he has offered Madeline. You must all play along with everything Odin says, while I try to figure out his agenda."

Erykah woke up in Alaric's arms and began to sniffle.

I was dying to take her, but we had to clear one thing up first.

"Why?" I asked. "Why are you so willing to help us?"

Loki's face was uncharacteristically serious as he replied, "Because I had children once too, and Odin did not do them any favors."

I was stunned as Alaric handed Erykah to me, then wrapped us both in his arms. He kissed the top of my head, but did not speak.

"I will leave you alone to process," Loki continued, still oddly morose. "Tomorrow we will begin to discuss our plan for remedying the magic leak in your world."

"You're going to help us with that too?" I blurted as he reached for the door.

He smirked. "Venture about with a glowing death ball and a thousand year old Viking intent on corralling age old magics and shoving them back up the World Tree? I wouldn't miss it."

I took a shaky breath. "Do you really think it can be done?"

He laughed. "I've learned to not question the possibilities where *you're* involved."

I smiled hesitantly, then looked down at Erykah. Maybe we *did* actually stand a chance. Maybe we could return things to normal and escape to our realm when our year was up. I would give it my all, but if it seemed like I was going to fail, or like Odin wasn't going to keep his end of the bargain, well he'd have a hell of a time finding Erykah after I spirited her away to Midgard, or perhaps some other realm beyond.

I remained wrapped in Alaric's arms as Loki exited the room. Faas set his tray of food down on the small table next to the chaise, then faced us.

"I'm sorry," he began, "but you're going to have to explain this all to me again. Don't tell me I'm going to be staying here to play nanny for a year."

"And don't tell me I'm supposed to wait here while you return to our realm and endanger yourself," Alaric added.

I looked down at Erykah in my arms. I was still nervous, but underneath that was quiet determination. Odin would not win, no matter what.

"What do you think?" I crooned, gazing at Erykah's plump face. "Should you tell them, or should I?"

Alaric sighed. "Please Madeline, this is serious."

I nodded, still looking down at my baby. "I know." I glanced between Faas and Sophie. "Could you guys give us a minute?"

Sophie scowled. "Fine, but I want a real explanation at some point too." She strode past me, grabbed Faas by the sleeve, then tugged him out of the room, closing the door behind them.

I sat on the chaise, cradling Erykah. "Hecate was sentenced to live out her life in a cell as a mortal," I said as Alaric sat beside me.

"What does that have to do with you being tasked to fix our realm?" he asked softly.

I shook my head. "There was no way I could get out of it. It was that, or the gods would have voted to kill me. At least this way, we stand a chance."

He gently stroked Erykah's dark hair. "And she must remain here?"

I nodded. "For now, at least until I figure something else out. And I need you to stay here with her. It's the only way I'll be able to bring myself to leave her."

He put his arms around me and kissed my cheek. "I'll stay, but I don't like you going up against wild magics."

I leaned into him. "I've faced immortals and necromancers, and I've even been possessed on more than one occasion, but none of it scared me as much as this. Not because of what I'll face, but because of what I stand to lose. I don't trust Odin."

"Nor do I," he replied, "but I trust you. It pains me to have to leave such a burden on your shoulders, but I will stay and protect our daughter, because I trust you to protect us all."

I turned into him, bringing my legs up as I held our daughter to my chest. He rocked us both gently, and I gave in to the moment. I gave into the feeling of being a mother with my wonderful partner by my side.

Tomorrow I'd worry about being a warrior. Today I'd just worry about being a mom. Or, I thought as my heart welled with fierce protectiveness, perhaps they were the same thing.

EPILOGUE

I walked down the silent hall in a burgundy tunic and soft black pants Freyja lent me, my boots clicking on the marble tiles. At least when I went home, I could retrieve some of my own clothes. Mikael had ventured back once to explain to Aila and the rest of the clan what was happening, but had come back empty handed, rushed and anxious to see Erykah.

One week had passed since I'd made my deal with Odin. It felt impossible to leave Erykah, but I needed to start my task. With so much to do, the year would go by quickly. In the morning Mikael and I would venture through the World Tree branch to Midgard. We'd begin our quest to contain the magics there, then would bring someone back with us, hopefully Tallie if she agreed, to help the others with Erykah.

I reached the end of the hall and turned, following the directions Freyja had given me. I wasn't sure why I felt compelled to visit Hecate in her cell, but something told me I needed to speak with her before I left. Perhaps it was just for closure, or perhaps to apologize. She may have deserved what she got, but she was still an ancient goddess. Her punishment seemed somehow wrong, even though I'd technically been the one to suggest it.

I reached the end of another hall and came upon two guards dressed in muted gray coats with brass buttons. Both appeared around my age, one with dark hair, and one red. Behind them was an iron-barred door. They both looked me up and down, then nodded.

"Goddess Freyja said to escort you inside," the dark-haired one said.

I stepped back as I realized he was the same guard I'd escaped that day after throwing porridge on Sif.

"No icy glasses of water today?" he asked with a smirk, his dark eyes glittering with good humor.

"Sorry about that," I muttered. "I was in a bit of a hurry to escape."

He chuckled as the other guard turned and unlocked the iron door, then held it open for us.

The dark-haired guard offered his arm to me. "I'm Morgan, by the way. I'm told you'll be staying with us for a while."

I slowly took his arm, wondering if he was secretly plotting revenge. "For a year," I replied, "though not by choice."

He nodded as he escorted me through the doorway.

We entered a torch-lined corridor with large prison cells along one side.

"Few of us choose to live in Asgard," he explained, "but we must do as the gods decree."

"So you're not a god?" I asked curiously, peering into each of the cells as we passed. A few held prisoners, but most were empty.

"Not even close," he replied with a laugh. "I hail from a realm not terribly different from Midgard. It was a small, rugged land, but I will always think of it as my home."

We reached another iron door, which he unlocked with a key from his belt.

"How did you end up here?" I asked without thinking, then added, "If you don't mind me asking."

"It's quite alright," he answered, "I've been gone from my realm long enough for the loss to no longer sting. I actually ended up here in much the same way as you."

I stopped walking down the seemingly endless hall of cells to blink up at him.

The corner of his lip quirked up in a smile. "No, I didn't bargain for a year to save my realm, but I *did* make a deal with one of the lesser gods. My wife was sick, and I pledged five hundred years of servitude for her to live."

"Five hundred years?" I questioned. "Are you immortal?"

He shrugged. "For now, I suppose. When my term is over I will be allowed to die, knowing my wife lived a long life with our children."

Well, *that* was sad. I shook my head. "But how were you able to make a deal with the gods without Yggdrasil to bridge the gap between worlds?"

"There's more than one way to travel between worlds," he said cryptically. We reached another door which he unlocked, then gestured for me to walk in ahead of him. "Take as long as you need. I'll be waiting right out here."

I stepped inside the torchlit space and the door soon shut behind me. This corridor only had one cell, with one occupant.

"I'm surprised you've come to see me," Hecate muttered.

Her cell was sparse, with only a lumpy looking bed, a small basin of water, and a chamberpot. She sat on the bed, slouching so that her auburn hair covered most of her face. Her white gown had been exchanged for a shapeless black tunic and loose pants. She had been my enemy, and still was, but it hurt my heart in some odd way to see her in such disgrace.

"I'm surprised too," I admitted. "I hadn't planned on it."

She pushed her hair out of her face as she looked up at me. "What do you want, Madeline? You have claimed my place on earth as your own. What could you possibly want from me now?"

"Odin has given me one year to clean up your mess," I explained. "I have to send all of the wild magics back from whence they came, or he will try to keep my child."

She let out a bitter laugh. "How poetic. You spurned my offer, an offer that would have seen you and your child safe *forever*, and instead put your faith in Odin. How does it feel to be screwed over by the gods? Not pleasant, is it?"

I scowled at her. "I shouldn't have come. I leave you to your eternity in a cell."

I began to reach for the door, then stopped as she snorted. "Not an eternity. You wanted me to be made human, remember? I'll probably die of pneumonia before terribly long."

I clenched my fist as I removed it from the door, then turned toward her. "You never should have killed those I loved. You and I could have found a compromise, but you refused to listen."

"It's as I expected then," she muttered. "You traveled back in time to stop me, didn't you? I never laid a finger on those you love, yet you seem to believe I have slighted you."

"You would have," I accused. "You *did*. They are only alive now because I stopped you before you could."

She stood and walked toward the bars of her cell, lacing her long fingers around them. Her green eyes were crazed as she replied, "Go ahead and tell yourself whatever helps you sleep at night. I will go to bed *happy* that I am not the one in a bargain with Odin. I would rather rot in this cell, than spend a year in his presence."

I narrowed my gaze at her. "What do you mean?"

She smirked. "Dear child, if you think you've made

any choices since you met Odin, you are wrong. Every step you make plays into whatever plan he has laid out for you. If he wants your child, he shall have her. You can eliminate every fleck of magic in your realm, and Odin will still take your child. She is as good as lost."

I felt tears welling behind my eyes, but refused to let them fall. Not in front of *her*.

My fists shook as I clenched them. "Goodbye, Hecate."

She smiled. "Goodbye for now, Madeline. I'm sure you'll be keeping me company in this cell before the year is through."

I turned away from her, flung open the door, then marched outside.

Morgan blinked at me, wide eyed. "Nice visit?"

"Fantastic," I grumbled, then marched onward as he locked the door behind me and caught up to my side.

He escorted me out from the remaining corridors in silence. As soon as I was out of his sight, I ran back toward my room, my boots echoing down the hall.

I only wished I could run farther.

THE MORNING after my visit with Hecate, Mikael, Loki, and I stood near the World Tree branch, prepared to venture back to Midgard. The others stood back a bit, here to see us off. After a little cajoling from Loki, Freyja had volunteered to help us in our quest as well, though she refused to come down with us until we had a concrete plan formulated. Our first recon mission was a waste of her valuable skills, in her own, humble opinion.

It was all well enough. I wasn't sure what we'd be arriving to, and I didn't mind Freyja staying behind to make sure no one tried to mess with Erykah. Faas was with the goddess now, giving her a lesson on how he manipulated energy.

I looked over at Erykah, cradled in Sophie's protective arms, with Alaric near, watching over his daughter. Erykah had turned out to be sweet-tempered beyond belief, rarely crying, and eating and sleeping without a fuss. The early birth hadn't seemed to cause any issues, and in fact, she seemed incredibly healthy. The Vaettir were a tough race, even from birth.

Leaving Loki and Mikael to grumble about what we should do first, I walked up to Alaric and Sophie.

Erykah gazed up at me with her stormy eyes. Her expression held a sense of *knowing* that I still couldn't comprehend. What I could comprehend was her magic. It was different from mine, like a crisp, clean light. There was no death magic in her, and no magic of war, which was odd given her lineage. If I were to choose just what her magic felt like, I'd say it felt like the Well of Urd, just like Faas had said. Pure, wild magic, contained within a tiny being. I couldn't help but consider that was why Odin wanted her.

With a dull ache in my heart, I kissed her forehead. *It's only for a day*, I assured myself. The plan was to return that evening. I would only be gone a day, so why did it feel like an eternity?

I forced a smile as I turned my gaze to Alaric. It felt like the fates were always separating us. It was painful, but at least we always managed to come back together. That's what really matters, I think, that through different realms and different timelines, we always came back together.

He wrapped me up in a fierce hug. "Be careful," he muttered.

"I always am," I joked as I pulled away, though I couldn't hide the tears in my eyes.

He kissed me gently, then pulled away, though there had been many more kisses, and much more fierce in the preceding days.

"Don't worry," Loki said as he walked up behind me. "I'll take *good* care of her." He threw an arm around my shoulders.

Alaric narrowed his dark eyes at him. "Why does that not make me feel any better?"

Mikael approached my back and put a hand on my shoulder as Loki let his arm fall away. "Are you ready?" he asked.

I took a deep, shaky breath, peering down at Erykah. "As I'll ever be."

After many more tears and drawn out goodbyes, I turned to face the World Tree branch. It was time for me to charge into battle with a red-haired god on one side, and an auburn-haired Viking on the other.

My heart felt like it was breaking as I reached a hand up to the branch, but still, I couldn't help the feeling that with my two mischievous companions, I rather liked my odds.

OUR FEET TOUCHED down on the soft sand beach of our realm. Tears burst forth from my eyes, and I would have fallen to my knees had Mikael not caught me.

"She will be safe," he whispered in my ear, helping me to stand. "You will see her again tonight."

I nodded, wiping at my tears as I pulled away to stand on my own. I blinked up at him, ignoring Loki waiting impatiently behind us.

"Thank you for coming with me," I muttered. "I don't think I would have had the strength to leave otherwise."

He put an arm around me. "You would have, that's what I love—" he cut himself off, then corrected, "what we *all* love about you."

"I know it's what *I* love about her," Loki joked.

I turned away from them both to hide my blush. I still didn't know what the hell I was going to do about Mikael. He and Alaric had formed a shaky truce because we all needed to focus on the task at hand, but that didn't change the fact that my heart was a total mess.

I blinked away the last of my tears, noticing a figure seated further down the beach, staring out at the tide.

His pure white hair hung slack down the back of his black shirt.

With Loki and Mikael following behind me, I approached him. "What are you doing here, Marcos?"

He looked up at me. "You tell me, Madeline. Hecate's presence has left my mind, and I feel I have lost some memories. I have waited here for days. It was the only place I could think to come to for answers."

My jaw fell. I'd only considered the timelines of myself and my closest companions, not everyone else. Marcos had likely been affected far more than others... not that I cared about his well-being, but it had to be confusing for him.

"Hecate has been made mortal," I explained, feeling awkward. "She will remain imprisoned in Asgard, the realm of the gods."

"So I am free?" he questioned.

I nodded.

His brow furrowed as he looked me up and down. "I can see you had your child. Is all well?"

I pursed my lips. This was...weird. Would he ask me about the weather next? "Er, yes," I replied. "All is well...enough."

Finally he stood, brushing the sand from his loose black pants.

"We should go," Mikael said from behind me.

He was right, but it seemed somehow wrong to just leave Marcos alone on the beach when he seemed so confused. He was evil, he'd killed the Norns, but he'd also been under the control of both Aislin and Hecate at that point.

"What will you do now?" I asked.

He tilted his head, observing me. "I'm not sure. What will *you* do?"

I glanced over my shoulder at Loki and Mikael, waiting not so patiently behind us. I had a cell phone in my pocket to call Aila to pick us up, but beyond that, we were just there that day to see how bad things have gotten.

"Do you know what's been happening here this past week?" I asked.

He nodded. "Pure chaos. The humans are up in arms, but they do not understand their foe."

"Madeline," Mikael said again.

Ignoring him, I said to Marcos, "Come with us, if you like. I'm sure this next year will be interesting."

A smile crept across his face. "Yes, that sounds like a fine plan."

"Oh Madeline," Mikael sighed, "must we pick up every stray?"

I turned to him with a smirk. "Hey, I gave you a chance, didn't I? And look how that turned out."

He glared at me for a moment, but seemed unable to resist the smile slowly forming on his lips.

"I'm hungry," Loki interrupted. "Can we find some food before we investigate?"

"We'll get some on the way," I assured, pulling the phone out of my pocket to call Aila.

I started walking as I powered on the phone, then scrolled through the contacts and selected her name. Mikael caught up on one side of me, and Loki on the other, while Marcos trailed behind.

I'd known there had been many possibilities for how motherhood would go, but in all my wildest dreams, I never could have imagined this.

The End

To keep track of new releases and updates, please visit:

www.saracroethle.com

Printed in Great
Britain
by Amazon